Praise for
Haven Jacobs Saves the Planet

"Once again, Barbara Dee has created vivid, real, likable middle school characters who tackle big problems. Full of humor, science, and activism, *Haven Jacobs Saves the Planet* addresses the eco-anxiety that many young people feel. Readers will cheer for Haven and her friends as they navigate complicated friendships and act to help save their town's river . . . and, just maybe, the planet."
—Rajani LaRocca, author of Newbery Honor Book
Red, White, and Whole

"Relatable, achingly imperfect, and inspiringly hopeful, Barbara Dee's characters jump off the page. Readers will cheer for Haven as she discovers that—in spite of our fears—we all have the ability to do small things greatly."
—Jodi Lynn Anderson, bestselling author
of *My Diary from the Edge of the World* and
the Thirteen Witches trilogy

"An empathetic exploration of youth eco-anxiety that provides comfort, hope, and ways to cope in an uncertain world. Barbara Dee's deeply developed and beautifully flawed characters navigate the ups and downs of friendships and family relationships as they face a local environmental crisis head-on in this crucial, timely, and engaging novel."
—Lisa McMann, *New York Times* bestselling author
of the Unwanteds series

"I loved this book! *Haven Jacobs* is full of heart, healing, and hope. This story will leave readers inspired, energized, and ready to change the world."
—Carrie Firestone, author of *Dress Coded*
and *The First Rule of Climate Club*

"Dynamic, engaging, and full of heart, *Haven Jacobs Saves the Planet* is the voice of a generation of kids who care deeply about the environment and want to put hope into action."
—Chris Baron, author of *All of Me* and *The Magical Imperfect*

"As readers keep turning the pages of this accessible and immediately engaging narrative, they will discover in Haven Jacobs a relatable, believable protagonist with an indefatigable spirit."
—Padma Venkatraman, author of *Born Behind Bars* and *The Bridge Home*

"A powerful and pitch-perfect story that will inspire readers to take action and fight for change."
—Alyson Gerber, author of *Taking Up Space* and *Focused*

Praise for
Violets Are Blue

"*Violets Are Blue* will break your heart and then piece it back together with infinite care. Barbara Dee expertly captures the struggle to be known and loved within a narrative that presents the complicated reality of addiction. Both Wren and her mother will stay with you long after this story is done."
—Jamie Sumner, author of *Roll with It* and *Tune It Out*

"Barbara Dee tunes into issues that impact middle schoolers and writes about them with compassion, insight, and just plain excellent storytelling. I loved this absorbing, accessible novel, which explores the heartbreaking effects of opioid addiction while also celebrating the joys of discovering a passion and finding people who understand you."
—Laurie Morrison, author of *Up for Air* and *Saint Ivy*

"Barbara Dee has done it again! *Violets Are Blue* is an emotionally rich story that masterfully weaves life's messy feelings while gently and thoughtfully tackling the difficult subject of opioid addiction. Beautiful. Complicated. And full of heart. A must read!"
—Elly Swartz, author of *Smart Cookie* and *Dear Student*

"Told realistically and with compassion, *Violets Are Blue* provides a fascinating look into the world of special effects makeup, budding friendships, family, and the secrets we keep."
—Melanie Sumrow, author of *The Inside Battle* and *The Prophet Calls*

An SLJ Best Book 2021
A Project LIT Book Club selection
A Junior Library Guild Selection
A Cybils Awards Finalist
One of A Mighty Girl's 2021 Books of the Year

Praise for
My Life in the Fish Tank

"I loved *My Life in the Fish Tank*. Once again, Barbara Dee writes about important topics with intelligence, nuance, and grace. She earned all the accolades for *Maybe He Just Likes You* and will earn them for *My Life in the Fish Tank* too."
—**Kimberly Brubaker Bradley, author of Newbery Honor Books**
Fighting Words* and *The War That Saved My Life

"I felt every beat of Zinny Manning's heart in this authentic and affecting story. Barbara Dee consistently has her finger on the pulse of her middle-grade audience. Outstanding!"
—**Leslie Connor, author of *A Home for Goddesses and Dogs* and National Book Award finalist *The Truth as Told by Mason Buttle***

"*My Life in the Fish Tank* is a powerful portrayal of a twelve-year-old dealing with her sibling's newly discovered mental illness. Author Barbara Dee deftly weaves in themes of friendship, family, and secrets, while also reminding us all to accept what we can't control. I truly loved every moment of this emotional and gripping novel, with its notes of hope that linger long after the last page."
—**Lindsay Currie, author of**
The Peculiar Incident on Shady Street* and *Scritch Scratch

"*My Life in the Fish Tank* rings true for its humor, insight, and honesty. Zinny is an appealing narrator, and her friendships with supporting characters are beautifully drawn."
—**Laura Shovan, author of *Takedown* and**
A Place at the Table

"Barbara Dee offers a deeply compassionate look at life for twelve-year-old Zinny, whose older brother faces mental health challenges. This touching novel will go a long way in providing understanding and empathy for young readers. Highly recommended."

—Donna Gephart, award-winning author of *Lily and Dunkin* and *Abby, Tried and True*

A Bank Street Best Book of the Year
A Junior Library Guild Selection
One of A Mighty Girl's 2020 Books of the Year

Praise for
Maybe He Just Likes You

"Mila is a finely drawn, sympathetic character dealing with a problem all too common in middle school. Readers will be cheering when she takes control! An important topic addressed in an age-appropriate way."
—Kimberly Brubaker Bradley, author of Newbery Honor Books
Fighting Words* and *The War That Saved My Life

"In *Maybe He Just Likes You*, Barbara Dee sensitively breaks down the nuances of a situation all too common in our culture—a girl not only being harassed, but not being listened to as she tries to ask for help. This well-crafted story validates Mila's anger, confusion, and fear, but also illuminates a pathway towards speaking up and speaking out. A vital read for both girls and boys."
—Veera Hiranandani, author of Newbery Honor Book *The Night Diary*

"Mila's journey will resonate with many readers, exploring a formative and common experience of early adolescence that has too often been ignored. Important and empowering."
—Ashley Herring Blake, author of Stonewall Children's & Young Adult Honor Book *Ivy Aberdeen's Letter to the World*

"*Maybe He Just Likes You* is an important, timeless story with funny, believable characters. Mila's situation is one that many readers will connect with. This book is sure to spark many productive conversations."
—Dusti Bowling, author of *Insignificant Events in the Life of a Cactus*

"In this masterful, relatable, and wholly unique story, Dee shows how one girl named Mila finds empowerment, strength, and courage within. I loved this book."
—Elly Swartz, author of *Smart Cookie* and *Dear Student*

"*Maybe He Just Likes You* is the perfect way to jump-start dialogue between boy and girl readers about respect and boundaries. This book is so good. So needed! I loved it!"
—Paula Chase, author of *So Done* and *Keeping It Real*

A Washington Post Best Children's Book
An ALA Notable Children's Book
A Project LIT Book Club selection
A Bank Street Best Book of the Year
An ALA Rise: A Feminist Book Project selection

ALSO BY BARBARA DEE

Violets Are Blue

My Life in the Fish Tank

Maybe He Just Likes You

Everything I Know About You

Halfway Normal

Star-Crossed

Truth or Dare

The (Almost) Perfect Guide to Imperfect Boys

Trauma Queen

This Is Me From Now On

Solving Zoe

Just Another Day in My Insanely Real Life

HAVEN JACOBS SAVES THE PLANET

BARBARA DEE

ALADDIN

NEW YORK LONDON TORONTO SYDNEY NEW DELHI

ALADDIN

An imprint of Simon & Schuster Children's Publishing Division
1230 Avenue of the Americas, New York, New York 10020
First Aladdin hardcover edition September 2022
Text copyright © 2022 by Barbara Dee
Jacket illustration copyright © 2022 by Erika Pajarillo
All rights reserved, including the right of reproduction in whole or in part in any form.
ALADDIN and related logo are registered trademarks of Simon & Schuster, Inc.
For information about special discounts for bulk purchases, please contact
Simon & Schuster Special Sales at 1-866-506-1949 or business@simonandschuster.com.
The Simon & Schuster Speakers Bureau can bring authors to your live event. For more
information or to book an event contact the Simon & Schuster Speakers Bureau
at 1-866-248-3049 or visit our website at www.simonspeakers.com.
Designed by Heather Palisi
The text of this book was set in Odile.
Manufactured in the United States of America 0822 FFG
2 4 6 8 10 9 7 5 3 1
Library of Congress Cataloging-in-Publication Data
Names: Dee, Barbara, author.
Title: Haven Jacobs saves the planet / by Barbara Dee.
Description: First Aladdin hardcover edition. | New York : Aladdin, 2022. | Audience:
Ages 9 to 13. | Summary: Twelve-year-old Haven channels her anxiety about the climate crisis
into a fight against the factory suspected of polluting the river running through her town.
Identifiers: LCCN 2021055549 (print) | LCCN 2021055550 (ebook) |
ISBN 9781534489837 (hc) | ISBN 9781534489851 (ebook)
Subjects: CYAC: Water—Pollution—Fiction. | Rivers—Fiction. | Anxiety—Fiction. | Middle
schools—Fiction. | Schools—Fiction. | BISAC: JUVENILE FICTION / Social Themes / General
(see also headings under Family) | JUVENILE FICTION / Science & Nature / Environment |
LCGFT: Novels.
Classification: LCC PZ7.D35867 Hav 2022 (print) | LCC PZ7.D35867 (ebook) |
DDC [Fic]—dc23
LC record available at https://lccn.loc.gov/2021055549
LC ebook record available at https://lccn.loc.gov/2021055550

For all kids everywhere who care about our planet.
Keep doing what you can. Keep speaking out.
"The future is inside us. It's not somewhere else."

HAVEN JACOBS SAVES THE PLANET

SENSITIVE

Sometimes in the middle of the night when I couldn't sleep, I'd think about the time I lost my family in a bouncy castle.

It happened at a state fair—a million years ago, when I was like four or five. We'd all been bouncing, having a great time, when suddenly my big brother, Carter, said his stomach felt funny. I watched my family race out of the castle, shouting for me to follow. But I wasn't ready to go, so I just kept on bouncing, all by myself.

Finally I stepped out of the castle to the flat, unbouncy ground, expecting to see Mom, Dad, and Carter.

BARBARA DEE

Except they weren't there.

No family.

For a second I froze, panicking. And then I started running.

I ran over to the Ferris wheel, then the roller coaster, then the ice cream stand where we'd all bought extra-large swirly cones an hour before. I ran over to a water-gun game where the prize was a giant stuffed Pikachu, then to the stage where some guy was playing a banjo, and past a lady in a cowgirl dress who was selling pies.

Somehow I made it back to the bouncy castle—and when I got there, my family was waiting. They looked terrified.

"Haven, what happened to you?" Dad yelled, and Mom burst into tears as she squeezed me tight.

"If you ever get separated from us, just stay put," she scolded when she finally stopped crying. "Promise you won't move around next time; let *us* find *you*."

I promised. But I remember thinking how silly that was. I mean, *of course* I'd try to find them! Because staying put just seemed so helpless and babyish. I needed to *do* something, not stand there waiting, like a stuffed Pikachu on a shelf.

"Haven's a true problem solver," Grandpa Aaron used to say.

"Yes, but not everything is a true problem," Mom would answer.

She'd talk to me about "learning to relax," "having patience," "accepting what we can't control." And Dad would talk about "enjoying the process." About "good sportsmanship," too, when I'd lose at *Blaster Force 3* to Carter or miss an easy goal in soccer.

"Haven, games are not about the final score," he'd tell me. "It's important to just have fun."

And I'd think: *Okay, but what's fun about losing?* To me, things counted only when I knew how they added up, or how they ended. So getting to the end of something—the solution of a puzzle, the last chapter in a book, the final scene in a movie—was basically why I was doing it in the first place.

I didn't try explaining this to Mom and Dad because I knew what they'd say: *Haven, honey, you should try to relax—enjoy the process!*

Although, to be fair, they didn't *only* talk this way, and sometimes they took my side. Like they did last summer, right before seventh grade, when our family went camping at Lake Exeter. I'd never gone fishing before, so I was excited to go out on the water with Dad and Carter. I even caught a trout in the first half hour.

Except the thing was, until the very second I caught

that trout, somehow I hadn't realized that catching a fish meant killing it.

"Can't we just throw it back?" I'd begged Dad.

"Come on, Haven, fish are food," Dad had replied.

"Not to me! I'm not a fish killer!"

Because how could I have eaten this creature that was still twitching and staring at me, that just a minute earlier I'd felt tugging on my rod? I absolutely couldn't. And I didn't want anyone else to eat it either.

"Aw, honey," Dad said to me. "Don't worry, fish don't have feelings."

"How do you know that?" By then I was almost crying.

Carter groaned. "Argh, Haven, why can't you just enjoy the lake! And being on this boat. You're missing the point of this whole vacation!"

"No, I'm not! Because the *point* of being on this boat is killing animals!"

"That's not the point at all! Why do you always have to make such a big deal about everything? And get so *emotional*?"

"All right, enough squabbling, you two," Dad said. "You'll scare off the other trout."

"Good, I hope we do," I said.

Right at that moment, without saying anything, Dad

threw the fish back. If he was annoyed with me, he didn't show it, but Carter did.

That night, as we ate a takeout supper back at our campsite, my brother announced, "I can't believe we came all the way here *to fish*, but because of Haven, we're eating ramen."

"Carter, you don't even like eating fish," Mom said. "And you love ramen! We all do," she added as she caught my eye.

Carter slurped some noodles. "Not the point. Haven's so hypersensitive. She can't relax about *anything*!"

"All right, Carter, you've shared your opinion; now let it go," Dad said sharply.

Mom changed the subject, but I didn't pay attention. Instead I was thinking how the lake was big, full of fish. Plenty of other people were still fishing. I'd saved the trout, but how much had I accomplished, really?

Plus I'd messed up my family's vacation, and now my brother was mad at me.

So even though I tried hard to enjoy myself—and the last few days of vacation before seventh grade—it felt like I'd won and lost at the same time.

ANTARCTICA

Of course I didn't say this to my brother, but even before that fishing trip I'd been thinking about bigger things than what we were eating for supper. I'd been thinking about the planet—all the scary stuff happening with climate change.

And not just thinking about it: worrying. Reading stories on my computer. Having bad dreams sometimes, like the one where a tornado tore the roof off our house. Another one about my favorite elm tree catching fire, and how I couldn't save a nest of baby robins. Another one about my bed floating away after a big rainstorm.

But I didn't talk about it, because I didn't want to hear how I was being "too sensitive," "too emotional," focusing on a problem-that-wasn't-really-a-problem.

Until one day in the spring of seventh grade, when our teacher Mr. Hendricks showed a video in science class. It was about Antarctica, how climate change was making the glaciers disappear.

At first I didn't get what the narrator was talking about, because he had an English accent and called them *glassy-ers*. But when I realized he meant *glay-shers*, and that they were melting in front of our eyes—right underneath the penguins—I got a funny buzzing feeling in my head.

If the glaciers melt, what happens to those penguins? I thought.

Don't ask me where this question came from. I mean, it wasn't like I was this penguin-obsessed person. I'd always *liked* penguins—the way they waddled and swam, the way both penguin parents took turns holding the eggs on their feet. But to be honest, I'd never really *thought* about them before.

And now this English guy in the video was talking about giant chunks of ice crashing into the ocean, meaning the Antarctic was in trouble. And that meant the penguins were in trouble, and probably the whales and the seals, too.

Also dolphins, right? Plus a million creatures and plants whose names I didn't even know.

Just then I remembered the trout, how we almost killed it for no good reason. And that made me think how humans were killing everything for no reason. How the whole planet—animals, plants, lakes, oceans, towns, cities—was in danger.

Including people. Including my family. And my friends.

Maybe our town would be swept up in a giant hurricane, and our school would sink. And our house would wash away while I was sleeping in my bed. Not just like in a scary dream, but *in real life*.

Suddenly I couldn't breathe. My chest got tight and I was sweating all over: my armpits, my hands, my scalp. One word flashed in my brain—*Run!*—and before I knew what I was doing, I ran out of the classroom to hide in the girls' restroom for the last four minutes of the period.

But even as I stood in front of the mirror, splashing cold water on my face, my brain kept replaying the video of that glacier crashing into the ocean, the penguins and other animals in danger. Like it was at the top of my mental playlist and I couldn't scroll past it. Or delete it. Or reboot.

At lunch my best friend, Riley, asked if I was all right. But it was hard to think of an answer that sounded normal.

"It's nothing," I said.

Riley's eyes were round and serious. "Come on, Haven. *Something's* going on; I can see it on your face. Just tell me, okay?"

I dipped a carrot stick in my hummus, making small circles. "Okay, so. It's that video we watched in science. It kind of freaked me out, actually."

"And that's why you left the room?"

I nodded.

"Yeah, I thought that was maybe it." Riley pulled the crust off her sandwich, making a crust pile on her napkin. "But how come it upset you so much? Because Mr. Hendricks is always showing us stuff like that, right?"

"Yeah," I admitted. "But this was different."

"Why?"

"I don't know, I just can't stop thinking about the penguins! Didn't it seem like they could almost *tell* the ice was melting under their feet? And that they couldn't do anything to stop it?"

"I guess," Riley said. "They do seem really smart, don't they? The way they communicate—"

"But it wasn't *just* the penguins. It was everything *else* in that video too. What's happening to the whales and dolphins. What's happening to Antarctica. An entire *continent*."

Riley blinked at me. I knew that lately she was scared

about her grandma's heart problems. If she was scared about climate stuff too, she'd never told me. And the truth was, we only talked about other stuff. School stuff, people stuff. Not this.

But now I couldn't shut up. "And it's not like we can go, 'Oh, it's Antarctica, a zillion miles away; it doesn't matter to us.' Because *of course* it does—climate change affects the whole planet! And we're all just sitting here, eating lunch, like *ho hum, just another boring school day.*"

Riley pushed away her sandwich and nibbled a chocolate chip off her cookie. "Okay, I'm not arguing with you, Haven. What are we supposed to do about it, though?"

"I'm not sure! But don't you think there has to be *something*? Because I hate just feeling so . . . helpless."

My voice was too loud, I could tell. A few tables over, Archer looked up at me. The two of us were still friends, I reminded myself, even if lately he'd been avoiding me at school.

"Okay if I sit here?" Without waiting for an answer, Ember Faraday was at our table, squeezing in next to Riley. "What are you talking about? You both look so *serious.*"

The way she said it was definitely a criticism.

I tried to catch Riley's eye. We used to have the same opinion of Ember, who everyone called Em. Before middle school she'd always acted like we had permanent head lice.

Then the big factory in town closed, her best friends' families moved away—and now, for some reason I didn't get, she'd started hanging out with Riley. Which meant hanging out with me.

I chewed what was left of my thumbnail.

"Oh, we're just talking about this video we saw in science," Riley told Em. Her whole face lit up, the way it always did when Ember Faraday was around. "Haven's pretty upset about it, so."

"Really?" Em smiled at me like I was a toddler. "How come, Haven?"

I switched to my pointer nail. "I don't know. Stuff about animals in danger always freaks me out, I guess."

"It was about Antarctica," Riley told her. "The melting glaciers, and what'll happen to all the penguins."

"Got it." Em pulled the top off her blueberry yogurt and licked the foil. "Okay, so tell me about this penguin video."

"It wasn't a *penguin video*," I said.

Em raised her eyebrows. "But penguins were *in* it?"

"A little. Mostly they were hiding from the camera." I looked at Riley to back me up, but she was playing with her crust pile.

"Wait, I don't understand," Em said. "Riley, didn't you say Haven was upset about—"

"The video was about climate change," I said through

my teeth. *"Not* just penguins. What it means for the *entire planet.* Including us."

"Oh. Well, *that's* depressing."

"Haven wants to do something to help," Riley explained.

Em licked a blob of purple yogurt off her spoon. "Like what, Haven? Another one of your projects?"

She meant the petition I'd started back in the fall to get more veggie food on the lunchroom menu. And the car wash I'd organized to raise money for the local SPCA. And possibly the bake sale I did with Riley in sixth grade to support an elephant sanctuary in Florida. We'd raised fifty-eight dollars, although half of that was from our parents.

"That's not what I mean," I said. "I just want to do something that *actually matters.*"

Now Em was giving me her *aren't you adorable* smile again.

"Well, I'm sure if anyone can save the planet, it's definitely *you,* Haven," she said.

THE SCRATCH

When I got home from school that afternoon, Carter, his best friend Gavin, and two other boys were playing basketball, the way they did every day that spring. I didn't know much about the other boys except that they were all freshmen at Belmont High School, which let out forty minutes ahead of Belmont Middle School. So after dismissal, I was used to finding Carter in our small driveway, shooting baskets at our rusty old hoop, sometimes with other boys, sometimes by himself.

Carter was hypercompetitive when it came to basketball, so he didn't stop dribbling to greet me. I waved at him anyway, then went inside, relieved to have the house to myself for a little while. Mom ran the Belmont Buddies Preschool in town; most days she wasn't home before five thirty. Neither was Dad, who was back at work again, finally, as a foreman at Gemba, the new glass factory in town. Well, *new* in the sense that eleven months ago Gemba took over the factory where Dad had worked before his old company moved out of Belmont and left him without a job for two and a half years.

In the kitchen I made myself my favorite after-school snack: Lucky Charms drowned in chocolate milk. I never ate this in front of my family, because they all said it was gross. But after six and a half hours of school, the cold crunchy sweetness was exactly what I needed.

By the time I finished and went upstairs to my bedroom, I could feel my neck muscles un-tensing. I loved being in my tiny room, with the piles of books on the faded green rug, the shells and rocks on the windowsill. On the wall next to my bed were two photos of me with Grandpa Aaron—one from when I was a baby, sitting in his lap, the other from the year he lived with us, just before he died. Next to those photos was a page I'd ripped out of a magazine, a picture of the Inuit teen climate activist Kirima Ansong, from the time she gave a speech at the United Nations. Sometimes people made fun of Kirima for stuttering, but she spoke so passionately about protecting the planet that when she finished that speech, they gave her a standing ovation.

Did Kirima Ansong know about the penguins? She seemed to know everything else about climate stuff, so I felt positive that she did.

I plopped on my bed, where our squishy, grumpy old cat Ziggy Stardust was asleep on my pillow, the way I usually found him when I got home from school. My family agreed that I was Ziggy's favorite person; whenever Carter teased me about it, Mom would say, "Well, cats aren't polite. They choose who they choose." And that always made me love Ziggy even more.

With the two unbitten nails of my left hand, I scritched his head while he yawned in my face. Ziggy's breath smelled like stinky fish, and it was funny to think that cats and penguins might have the same sort of fishy-breath smell. Ziggy wasn't anti-bird—at least, I never saw him attack any through the windows—but still, he'd probably be offended if you told him they had stuff in common, like a taste for fish.

Although maybe we all had stuff in common with penguins. Maybe we were all standing on shrinking ice. Knowing it was shrinking, and not knowing what to do about it. If there was even anything we could do at all.

Right that second, Ziggy decided he'd had enough head-scritching, and stabbed my wrist with a too-pointy claw.

"Yeow!" I shouted.

He widened his eyes like, *Innocent little me? What did I do?*

"You know exactly," I told him as I headed to the bathroom, where I ran cold water on the scratch to stop the bleeding. Although I wasn't actually mad at Ziggy, because how could you be? Cats scratched: it was who they were, and if you loved them, you had to accept that. Although you *could* stop the head-scritching a second or two before they'd had enough. You just had to pay attention to your cat's feelings, which I obviously hadn't.

When the bleeding stopped, I blotted my arm with some tissue, then peeked at myself in the mirror. People said I showed all my feelings on my face—but was that true? *All* my feelings? Sometimes it felt like I had so many feelings, I needed a truck to lug them around behind me.

I made a sad face. A happy face. A surprised face. Was this what people saw when they looked at me? All I saw was a droopy brown ponytail, brown eyes with thin brown eyelashes, pale cheeks, and four tiny pinkish spots on my forehead. A sort of zit constellation. Bleh. Em had so many freckles you couldn't tell if she had a zit, and Riley's dark brown skin practically glowed. Why was I the only one with skin issues?

I washed my face with extra soap, tossed Ziggy one of his chewed-up catnip socks, then went to my desk to turn on my laptop. And it wasn't like I had the specific thought, *Okay, and now I'm going to read scary articles about Antarctica.* I just couldn't help it.

> *The Doomsday Glacier, the most*
> *important glacier in the world, is melting—*
> *Twelve million penguins endangered—*
> *Humpback whales, leopard seals—*
> *Scientists alarmed—*
> *Greenhouse gases—*
> *Melting sea ice—*
> *Record high temperatures also recorded*
> *in Alaska—*

"*Haven.*" My brother had opened my door, looking sweaty and annoyed. "Didn't you hear the phone just now?"

"What? No, sorry," I said, pulling out my earbuds.

"Well, it was Mom. She stopped to buy groceries on her way home from work. She said she tried the landline but nobody answered, so she called me. Just as I was about to tie the score." He wiped his sweaty brow with the back of his hand. "What're you watching?"

"Nothing." I shut my laptop. "I was just reading some stuff. For school."

"With the door closed? And with earbuds?"

"Some of the articles had videos."

"Uh-huh. I totally believe you." He grinned. "Well, have fun with your *homework*."

I could feel my cheeks heating. "Carter, I don't care what you think. But it's for my science class, okay?"

"Sure," Carter said. He was already down the hall. "Whatever you say, Lentil."

GERMS

fter the trout incident last summer, I'd turned vegetarian—because it was a decision I could make, something specific I could do. And that was when my brother started calling me "Lentil," although only when our parents weren't around to make him stop.

"You know, Lentil," he'd say, "the whole world isn't about *you*. And your sensitive feelings."

"I'm not saying it is," I'd reply, trying to keep my voice as calm as possible.

"Well, people are still going to catch fish and grill

hamburgers. So you cooking beans won't solve anything. Or even matter."

There was no point informing my brother that lentils were legumes, not beans, so I'd just shrug. And it wasn't like I thought lentils were magic, or that if I ate some for supper, poof, no more climate change. But I told myself that going veggie was good for the planet, no matter what Carter said. Plus, of course, it was kinder to animals. So maybe changing my food was a teeny thing, not some major accomplishment or solution—but it still made a difference in the world, right? And probably it was the most that I could personally do, anyhow.

Mom loved to watch cooking shows, but she didn't enjoy making supper. This meant I was the one trying veggie recipes I found online, like lavender-honey muffins (which tasted a bit like soap) and lentil chili (so spicy it made me sweat, but not in a bad way). Sometimes my family ate this food; sometimes they didn't. Seriously, I didn't care which. Because even when the food turned out terrible, it still felt good taking something out of the oven, or off the stove—something I'd made with my own hands. And if all my work disappeared as soon as you ate it, that was the whole idea.

Over the weekend I'd made a big batch of chickpea balls, and now we were all eating them with spaghetti and tomato sauce. Dad was telling Mom about some new project at Gemba, etching glass with acid to make it look "frosted." Mom was happy because Belmont Buddies had just signed up three more preschoolers, all of them the kids of new Gemba workers. And Carter was talking about whatever Carter talked about; I couldn't follow, and to be honest, I didn't try.

"You're not eating much tonight," Dad said suddenly. It took a second to realize he meant me.

"Yeah, I don't know," I said. "I guess I'm not hungry."

"But these meatballs are so delicious," Mom said. She was always the one who seemed extra enthusiastic whenever I cooked anything, probably because it meant she didn't have to.

"You think so? They're not too chewy?" I asked.

"Oh, not at all! Anyhow, I *like* them chewy."

"So do I," Dad said. "Nobody likes mushy meatballs."

"Although technically they're not *meatballs*," Carter said.

"Not true," I said. "'Meatball' isn't literally *a ball of meat*."

"Of *course* it is, Haven! Just like 'snowball' is literally *a ball of snow*."

"Yeah, well, 'football' isn't literally *a ball of feet*. And 'mothballs' aren't made out of moths!"

21

"Okay, fine, but *hairballs*—"

"*All right,*" Dad said. "Do we really need the two of you squabbling at every single meal?" I could tell he realized he sounded harsh, because he took a breath, then changed his voice. "So why *aren't* you eating, Haven?"

Maybe I could have made up some excuse. (*Too much social studies homework! Riley's new friend Em! Archer avoiding me at school!*) But for some reason I explained about the video we saw in science, how all day I couldn't stop thinking about Antarctica and the penguins. And just now I'd found out about something called the Doomsday Glacier. So thinking about the end of our planet kind of, you know, spoiled my appetite.

Carter stuffed a chickpea meatball in his mouth and talked anyway. "Yeah, and you know what we learned in earth science today? A lot of the planet is permafrost, which is just a bunch of ice and rocks and soil all frozen together, right? It's underneath everything, buildings and roads and pipelines and stuff. And now it's thawing really fast, especially in the Arctic."

"The Arctic?" I rubbed my Ziggy scratch. "So that endangers polar bears?"

"Yeah, but not only polar bears—also millions of people who live in Siberia! And it means greenhouse gases and wildfires for the rest of the world. Oh, wait, listen to this:

when the permafrost thaws, so do prehistoric germs!"

"Prehistoric germs?"

"Uh-huh. Bacteria and viruses that were trapped in the ice! For centuries! And now are released into the atmosphere! Doesn't that sound sci-fi? But it's science *fact*."

Carter's words gave me a sweaty, tingly feeling. Because it was like: *Scientists know about these other germs, we have medicine and vaccines, we know what to do, but hey, here's a scary ancient germ we've never even seen before!* And if climate change meant even *more* scary germs like from dinosaur times, how would we all survive?

"Enough, Carter," Dad said. "Haven doesn't need to hear that. *None* of us do."

"But Dad, I *want* to hear it," I said. "It's extremely important!"

"Dino germs are important to you, Hay? Since when?" Dad smiled at me, but I didn't smile back.

"Haven, honey, please try to relax," Mom said. "And Carter, last I checked, Belmont isn't melting."

"That's not the *point*, Mom," Carter said. "Climate change is about the whole planet! And nature is all connected, so if something happens somewhere else, it still affects Belmont."

I knew my brother was smart, and also a very good student, so it didn't shock me that he knew this stuff. What shocked me was that for once he wasn't teasing me. Or acting like I was "being too sensitive" or "missing the point" about things.

"I agree with Carter," I said quickly. "It *does* affect us. All of it does! And it's really, really serious!"

My brother raised his chin at me. Our eyes met.

"No one's disagreeing." Mom sighed. "It's a very important topic. But this has been a long, stressful day at work, guys. I'm tired, and I know Dad is too. So can we *please* not have upsetting conversations at the dinner table?"

I looked at my parents. Actually, they did seem tired. Exhausted, really. I knew Dad was relieved to have a job again, but he had purple-gray shadows under his eyes. Mom's mouth had extra wrinkles in the corners—how had I not noticed before?—and her hair looked heavy and faded, like she'd missed a salon appointment. Maybe two.

"Sorry," I said.

"Fine," Carter muttered.

Right away my parents started talking about a funny sound the car was making, and how we should probably think about replacing the water heater, so which one should we take care of first? Now that Dad was back at work, we had money to spend on repairs, but we couldn't afford them all at once, so we had to decide which was the bigger emergency.

At least that's what I think they were talking about; I spaced out after a minute.

Carter got quiet too. But after supper was over, as we were loading our dishes in the dishwasher, he turned to me.

"You know, I wasn't joking about the prehistoric germs," he said.

"I never thought you were," I replied.

THE LETTER O

That night, as I cuddled in my bed with Ziggy, I heard the sound of ice cracking, splashing into the ocean.

Penguins crying. Whales calling for help. Polar bears too.

The permafrost thawing. Did it make a sound deep beneath the surface of the earth?

And did prehistoric germs make a whooshing sound when they escaped into the air?

Maybe things were happening and we didn't even know, because there was no video. Or audio. Or witnesses.

What was that question? *If a tree falls in a forest and no*

one is around to hear it, does it make a sound? How much was silent and invisible? But also real?

Maybe by the time we found out, everything would be gone, including Belmont. Including this house. Including this bed.

And it would be too late to save any of it.

An hour after I got into bed that night, it was like my brain was a bouncy castle, and these thoughts wouldn't stop jumping and crashing into each other. So I did my usual tricks for whenever I couldn't sleep: I fluffed my pillow. I drank some water. I counted to one hundred by prime numbers. None of it helped—not even smooshing my face into Ziggy's fur while he made creaky old-cat-sleeping noises.

As a last resort I played this game I'd invented a few months ago, after one of my floating-away-bed nightmares. The way the game worked was that you picked a letter from the alphabet—today it was *O*—and pretended that for the rest of your life you could eat only foods starting with that letter.

That meant I could eat Oreos, oatmeal, oatmeal cookies (because they counted as a separate food), okra, olives, olive oil, onions, oranges, orange juice. Oysters, if I ate shellfish, which I didn't. Omelets, because I still ate eggs— although lately I'd been wondering if I should go vegan.

Not much of a menu, really.

After about fifteen minutes I gave up on the letter *O* and took out my phone. Sometime late last night Archer had texted me. Hey did you ever check out that game I told you about? RoboRaptors. So bad it's actually good, right?

Not yet, sorry, I texted back. *Too busy freaking about the planet, Archer. And why can't we have this conversation in real life? In the lunchroom at school, the way we used to?*

At around midnight I turned on my computer, chewed what was left of my pinky nails, and watched penguin videos.

GREAT BARRIER REEF

*T*he next morning while I was walking to school, I got two texts. The first was from Archer, replying to my reply about the *RoboRaptors* game. Yeah, I got stuck on Level 3 but then I figured out how to use the laser . . .

He went on explaining how he captured a crow's nest. I didn't need all that detail for a game I wasn't even playing, so I just texted back a smiley face—not a big smile, just a sort of neutral one. Like: *Huh, cool. Glad you're having fun.*

The second text was from Riley. !!! Newboy Kenji!!!

Sometimes Riley's texts were hard to figure out. She used abbreviations no one else did, like *mayb* for "maybe"

and *2w* for "tomorrow"; so possibly *newboy* was short for something.

Although I could guess what she meant. A few weeks ago our homeroom teacher told us we'd be getting a new kid in our class named Kenji Stillman. This was a big deal for two reasons: first, because he was coming all the way from Australia, and second, because he was coming from anywhere. Since the old factory shut down, we were used to people moving away, but hardly anyone ever moved *to* Belmont these days. Because, seriously, why would they?

YEAH JUST GOT HERE!! Riley texted. Adljgdlkgjd SOOO CUUUTE <3 !!! Whr r u???

On my way, I replied, wondering how cute you had to be to earn caps plus all those extra letters and punctuation.

As soon as I took my seat in homeroom, I could tell two things about this boy: first, that Tabitha Kim had claimed him, and second, that he wasn't happy about it. He sat hunched over, like he was defending himself from spitballs.

"I'll give Kenji a tour," Tabitha announced as the bell rang for first period.

He looked up, finally, so I could see his face. Thick brown hair that fell in his eyes, high cheekbones, mouth that seemed ready to smile. Olive skin with zero zit constellations—at least none detectable from across the room.

Oh, I thought. Because he was the cutest boy I'd ever seen in real life, actually.

It was hard to look at him. And hard not to look.

"Why do I need a tour?" he was asking. His voice sounded American, not Australian.

"Why?" Tabitha flipped her long black hair. "Oh, because trust me, Kenji, this building is *impossible!* There's a north wing and a south wing, but you can't tell which wing you're in from the room numbers. Plus there's a new lunchroom and an old one, but you can't get to the new one unless you know which staircase—"

"That's okay, I'll figure it out," Kenji said.

"Well, if you have any questions, just ask!"

"'Kay, thanks," Kenji said, typing on his phone. He wasn't being mean, I thought; he was actually being super polite. But it was the kind of polite that meant you should back off.

I tried to catch Riley's eye, but she was staring at Kenji.

One thing about me: all my crushes were secret, even from Riley. She would tell me who she liked, who she stopped liking, who she maybe liked a little. Since the beginning of fifth grade, when we first became friends, she was constantly talking and texting about this topic. But she wasn't looking for clues about whether the boy liked her back; it was more about liking than about being liked.

The boys she picked for crushes were loud and sports-obsessed—younger versions of my brother, basically. So I never told her who *I* liked, because what if she didn't understand? My crushes were the quiet boys, the smart ones: Rafael, who could multiply three-digit numbers in his head. Ishaan, who kept a stack of Magic: The Gathering cards in his backpack.

But not Archer, by the way. He was never a crush, always just a friend. Even if one day he'd decided we shouldn't hang out with each other at school. Or be in public together, for that matter.

What I'm saying is, I could look at a boy like Kenji, see that he was cute—I mean, *really cute*—and not for a second consider him crush material. The way I thought about it, you couldn't be that cute without knowing it. And if you knew it, that meant you were conceited, and therefore you didn't deserve a crush. Plus, the way other girls were staring at him, giggling, the way Tabitha Kim was pouncing like he was one of Ziggy's catnip socks—it was too much to deal with, especially today, when my brain was swirly and fuzzy from not sleeping. Besides, I had more important things on my mind, like the Doomsday Glacier.

So I decided to ignore this new boy as much as possible, even though I kept spotting him with Archer. And with other smart boys like Ishaan and Rafael.

The ignoring went okay until lunch, when all of a sudden he and Archer were standing right in front of us, both of them balancing trays of too much food. Archer looked queasy, like he couldn't believe Kenji had actually led him to our table. Where I was sitting, eating a grilled cheese sandwich.

"You saving these seats?" Kenji asked. I shook my head, avoiding eye contact with Archer.

"Oh, of course not," Riley said eagerly. "You can't reserve seats in the lunchroom!"

"Just wanted to be sure," Kenji said as he lowered his tray onto the table. "Didn't know if you were waiting for someone."

Riley's eyes met mine. Then I saw her text someone under the table. I couldn't see who, but I could guess.

She looked up and smiled. "So Kenji," she said brightly. "What do you think of school so far?"

"This place? I dunno." He shrugged.

"Hey, thanks," Archer said. "Glad we made such a strong impression."

"No, no. I just mean I've been to a lot of schools. This one seems pretty . . . regular."

Was that good or bad? It was hard to think of "regular" as a compliment.

I didn't know what to say or where to look, so I focused on the melted cheese in my sandwich.

And now Em was squeezing in next to Riley. She didn't seem surprised to find Kenji sitting with us, which meant I'd guessed right about who Riley was texting.

Maybe because the table had gotten so crowded, I suddenly felt hyperaware of my body, especially my Ziggy scratch, which was starting to bother me. Not in a mosquito-bite sort of way; it was more like a dull-but-impossible-to-ignore low-key itch. But with hardly any fingernails left, I just rubbed it through my sleeve while I ate my sandwich.

"Why have you been to a lot of schools?" Riley was asking Kenji.

He sipped some water. "My dad travels around for business. Like a year in one place, a year somewhere else. And my family has to go with him, so."

"Whoa, lucky," Riley said. "Our family never goes any-where."

"It's okay. Mostly." Kenji examined the pasta on his fork like it was an exotic species he'd never seen before. "I'm American, even though I was born in Tokyo. So far I've been to school in Germany, Indonesia, South Africa, Japan, and Australia. Although I did kindergarten in Ohio."

"And now here you are in beautiful Belmont," Archer said, rolling his eyes.

"Hey, Archer, I like Belmont," Riley said.

Archer snorted. "You *do*? Why?"

"Oh, come on." Riley turned to smile at Kenji. "Belmont's so much better than a few years ago. It was basically *dead* when the old factory closed. Now there's a bakery and a pizza place."

"And a barber shop and a nail salon," Archer said. "Wait, no—*two* barber shops. Oh, and for late-night excitement, a hardware store."

I couldn't help looking at him then. Archer didn't even sound like Archer. He sounded . . . older. Snarky. Almost like he was trying to imitate Carter.

Why was he acting so strange all of a sudden?

Em was making her mouth into a little pout. "So *anyway*, Kenji. Of every country you've been to, which is your favorite?" It sounded like she was interviewing him, and we were the audience.

"I dunno, maybe Australia?" Kenji said. "But the bushfires were incredibly scary. Like a billion animals died, including koalas. And now what's happening to the Great Barrier Reef . . . I can't stop thinking about it. It's really bad."

"What do you mean?" I asked.

Kenji turned to me and blinked. "You don't *know*?"

He didn't say it in a stuck-up way, more like he was surprised at my answer. And the thing was, I had the feeling

I'd read something somewhere, or seen something online. But if I acted like I actually knew, I might say something wrong.

I could feel my cheeks burning as I shook my head. Why did I even care what this boy thought?

Kenji chewed some pasta. "Well, but you *should* know," he said. "*Everyone* should. They're killing the coral, and that endangers dolphins. Other animals too."

"Oh, Haven's fine with *that*, then," Em said, smirking. "She only cares about penguins!"

"Not funny," I snapped.

I could tell my voice was too loud. Which was probably why everyone was staring at me, including Riley. And why Em's face had scrunched up.

But no. That wasn't why.

"Haven, omigod, your *arm*," she was saying.

My arm? "What about it?"

"It's bleeding! Are you okay?" Riley's eyes bugged.

I looked down: the forearm of my sleeve had a slug-shaped stain, about the size of a quarter. A melting quarter.

Ew.

"It's nothing," I said quickly. "Just a cat scratch from yesterday. I must have rubbed off the scab by accident."

"Well, you definitely need a Band-Aid!" Riley said. "Want me to come with you to the nurse?"

I shook my head.

Riley turned to Em. "Wait, don't you have Band-Aids in your locker? I'm sure I saw some."

"I might," Em admitted. She didn't seem too enthusiastic. "We could look."

Because I couldn't think of an argument, I followed her out of the lunchroom.

LOCKER

Em led me to her locker, which was the opposite of mine in every way. I knew some girls (for example, Riley) decorated their lockers with stickers and photos and fancy calendars, but not me. I used mine for dumping my jacket, and maybe a notebook or two, but that was it. I never made it all cute and cozy, because what was the point? It wasn't like I'd move in.

Em's locker was way past cute and cozy. The door was covered in cupcake-themed gift wrap, and inside she'd hung a mirror with a fuzzy pink frame, a flower-shaped whiteboard, and a calendar with horse-of-the-month photos. The top shelf was lined with three small baskets with different-colored ribbons—a red ribbon for pens and pencils, a blue one for snacks, a green one for other stuff I couldn't see.

She grabbed the Other Stuff basket. "I *think* I have a few Band-Aids here somewhere—oh wait, here they are! And antiseptic spray! You'd better use that first."

"Thanks," I said. She was acting nice, but I didn't trust her.

She watched, frowning, while I sprayed and bandaged my arm. Even making a face like this, Ember Faraday was pretty. Pretty hazel eyes, pretty light brown hair. Even her freckles were pretty. In fact, it wasn't possible to imagine her ever having a not-pretty day, with a floppy ponytail and zit constellations.

"Haven, can I say something?" she asked. "I don't understand how you didn't even *know* you'd picked off that scab."

I shrugged. "Because it didn't hurt. It was just a little itchy."

"And your nails."

Was that a question? "What about them?"

"I mean, no offense, but why do they look like that? I know plenty of people who bite, but yours are, like, out of control."

A cold wave passed over me.

"I've been noticing them for a while now," she continued.

"And I didn't want to embarrass you in front of Riley, so I never said anything. But lately they look even worse. Are you . . . okay?"

"I'm fine," I said. "It's just a nervous habit."

"Really?" She blinked sympathetically. "What are you nervous about?"

The permafrost melting. Everything collapsing and disappearing.

Animals in danger. Wildfires and floods. Prehistoric germs.

The way Archer won't even look at me.

This cute new boy.

You.

"Just a bunch of random things," I said.

"So have you tried a rubber band?"

"Excuse me?"

"To wear on your wrist. Instead of biting your nails, you snap it. It really works, I swear."

"Okay, thanks," I said.

Was she mocking me? It was hard to think anything else.

The bell rang.

"Thanks for the suggestion. And the Band-Aid," I said over my shoulder.

Then, instead of going to social studies, I went to the girls' restroom, locked myself in a stall, and typed *Great Barrier Reef* on my phone.

LEWIS AND CLARK

*T*he thing about researching climate things: once you started, it was impossible to stop. Every article about the Great Barrier Reef led you to a million other articles. Sometimes you had to click around a little to figure out which ones were real and which were just some random person's opinion, but all of them made it hard to breathe.

Fifty percent of coral lost due to climate change–
Home to dwarf mink whales, humpback dolphins, 1,500 fish species, crocodiles, sea

turtles, sharks, stingrays, mollusks, more than
2,000 species of plants—
  Coral can't keep up with rising water
temperatures—

The more I read, the stranger I felt. My head buzzed. I was hot and cold, sweaty and shaky. My stomach hurt too—and then, all of a sudden, I had an attack of diarrhea.

Gross, I thought. *At least I have the bathroom to myself. But gross.*

I washed my hands at the sink, then went back to my phone. None of the articles had any suggestions for solving the problem of the Great Barrier Reef. Even so, I kept reading. Staring at photos and videos. I even watched a video of Kirima Ansong from last year, the time she spoke to the United Nations. Turning off my phone, going to class, didn't even cross my mind.

Finally two eighth-grade girls walked into the bathroom. They were talking about some other girl's outfit, laughing in a loud, not-nice way I couldn't ignore.

So I slipped my phone into my pocket, splashed some freezing-cold water on my face, checked for new zits (none, phew), and went down the hall to social studies.

Immediately I realized this was a mistake. The class

was hunched over papers, scribbling and sighing. Taking a test I'd totally forgotten about.

Crap.

Our teacher, Ms. Packer, was at her computer in the back of the room. As soon as she saw me at the door, she hurried over.

"Haven, you all right?" she asked quietly.

"Yeah." I slipped my hands in my pockets so she wouldn't see my fingernails. "I felt funny before, but I'm better now."

"Okay, good. Riley said you weren't well at lunch, and I was worried. The period's more than half over; just answer as many questions as you can." She gave me an encouraging little smile as she handed me a test.

I took it to my desk. Riley looked at me with question-mark eyes, so I did a quick thumbs-up.

What was the main goal of Lewis and Clark's expedition?

What was the significance of the Louisiana Purchase?

What were three factors that led to the War of 1812?

Twenty questions bobbed up and down on the page like swim toys in the ocean. Even if I had studied, which I hadn't, my brain couldn't stop the bobbing.

All I could think was: *The Great Barrier Reef is dying. The whole planet is melting, burning, on fire.*

I have to do something. Say something. Anything.

At the bottom of the page I wrote an answer, the only one I could think of, the only one that mattered in the actual world:

Who cares? Why are we studying this? We should talk about climate change!!

THE BLANKS

Once in fourth grade our teacher told us to study for a test on magnetism. It was Carter's birthday; we went out to a diner for supper, then had birthday cake back home. By the time he opened his presents, I'd forgotten all about the magnetism test, and anyway it was too late to study.

At school the next morning, I left about half the test blank. So of course I failed, and my teacher said I had to get it signed by a parent.

Grandpa Aaron was living with us then. After Mom signed my test, lecturing me about personal responsibility, he put his bony arm around my shoulders.

"Let me give you some advice, Haven," he said as he stroked my cheek. "Always answer every question."

"But how could I if I didn't study?" I protested.

"Makes no difference." He winked at me. "Answer anyway. Use all the words you can think of. A bad answer can earn you a few points, but a blank answer earns nothing."

I figured he was right about this. Not just because Grandpa Aaron was kind of a hero to me, the way he'd climbed mountains and explored caves when he was younger. Also because he got who I was—how much I needed to feel like I'd solved a puzzle, finished a job, accomplished something. Gotten good grades, even when I hadn't studied.

What I'm saying is, at the moment I wrote that answer at the bottom of Ms. Packer's test, it felt like I had no choice. But that night, instead of sleeping, I started worrying. What had I done? What if Ms. Packer thought I'd been disrespectful? I knew it wasn't *her* fault that we were studying pointless topics; she was a cool person with long locs and a rainbow wrist tattoo that looked amazing on her brown skin. I knew she cared about things like Black Lives Matter and Pride because she showed us photos of herself at marches.

Really, I should have just followed Grandpa Aaron's advice. Written anything. Filled in the blanks with bad answers: *Lewis and Clark, blahblahblah.*

Because how did leaving my test blank save the planet? It didn't.

It didn't accomplish anything, except getting me in trouble, probably.

Two days later, Ms. Packer met me in the hallway before the start of class.

"So I read your test last night," she said.

She was waiting for me to say something. But when I opened my mouth, nothing came out.

"Is everything okay, Haven?" she asked, searching my face.

"Yeah." I stuffed my hands in my pockets. "Everything's fine."

"Really?" She waited again. "Because I've noticed you've been very distracted in class lately. I'm missing three of your last homework assignments. And now there's this unit test, which obviously I can't grade."

If she'd said it in a mean or shouty way, I'd probably have shrugged or something. But her voice was gentle and her eyes were soft.

"I'm really sorry." I could hear I sounded a little shaky. "It's just hard to focus right now."

"How come?"

"I don't know. I keep . . . thinking about things."

"Oh, honey," she said. Middle school teachers hardly ever called you "honey," especially young ones like Ms. Packer, so hearing that word made me catch my breath. "Can you tell me what you're thinking about?"

Could I? I wasn't sure. Maybe I could.

"It's a lot of things," I admitted. "Some stuff with my friends lately. But mostly it's what I wrote on the test. It just feels like school is—I don't know, sort of pointless, really. Because the planet is in danger, animals are dying, and nobody's doing anything to stop it." I felt my Ziggy scab under the Band-Aid I was still wearing. *Don't you want to scratch me?* it was calling. *Not now,* I answered.

"I hear you." Ms. Packer nodded slowly. "The climate crisis is a huge issue, and it's easy to feel overwhelmed. But can I ask where you're getting your information?"

"Different places. The internet, mostly. I've been reading a lot, but there's just so much!"

"Okay, but what are your sources? Not everything on the internet is true, you know. Are you reading things by actual climate scientists?"

"I'm trying. But some of those articles are incredibly complicated. Also Mr. Hendricks keeps showing us videos."

"About the climate crisis?"

"Yeah." I pressed on the Band-Aid to make the scab shut up.

"Have you told him these videos are upsetting you?"

"No. I mean, they're *supposed* to, aren't they? Because we *should* be upset."

"Yes, I'm sure that's right." Ms. Packer looked like she was thinking about what to say next as she pushed a loc behind her ear. "But what I can tell you from my own experience is that there's a positive way to be upset, and another way that just makes you feel hopeless and depressed. And I think about a quote attributed to Dr. King: 'If I cannot do great things, I can do small things in a great way.' So I always aim to do small things."

But what good is a small thing? When the problem is so big?

"Okay, thanks," I said.

Was Ms. Packer reading my mind? She didn't take her eyes off my face. "What I tell myself is that I can't fix the whole world, but I can have a local impact, you know? Also, I try to identify allies—people who aren't necessarily my friends, but who feel the same as I do about issues. Allies are really important, Haven."

"I know. I mean, yes, I agree."

Now she smiled. "Has Mr. Hendricks mentioned the River Project?"

I could hear the capital letters in her voice.

I shook my head.

"Well, ask him about it, okay? It should be coming up pretty soon; he does it with the seventh grade every spring. I think focusing on something right here in town may make a big difference for you. And I think getting out of this building, being hands-on with the Belmont River, could really help."

I wondered what she meant by the word "help." Because even if we studied the Belmont River—which sounded cool, I had to admit—what did that have to do with saving the planet? It seemed like a bad answer, not much better than a blank.

But I desperately needed to trust somebody—any grown-up at all. And why shouldn't it be Ms. Packer?

"Okay," I said, although I wasn't agreeing to anything specific.

"All right, then. And Haven?" Ms. Packer fluttered my test paper. "I'll ignore this test, but it's a one-time deal. Next time you have to answer the questions. *And* you need to turn in that missing homework."

Of course I promised.

CHEMICALS

After that conversation with Ms. Packer, I did feel a microscopic bit better. Because at least I wasn't in trouble with her, and I wouldn't have to ask my parents to sign a failing test.

But I didn't rush off to see Mr. Hendricks, because the truth was, I was scared to talk to him.

Not that I didn't like him; I did. In fact, Ms. Packer and Mr. Hendricks were my two favorite teachers, but for opposite reasons. Ms. Packer was someone I could imagine caring about non-school things: walking her dog, eating pizza, going on protest marches with her friends. But when it came to Mr. Hendricks, my imagination crashed. Everything about him—his dorky black glasses, his inside-the-building paleness, his teacher-joke tees (NEVER TRUST AN ATOM—THEY MAKE UP EVERYTHING)—made me think he was basically Mr. Science, even on weekends. Did he have a family? A pet? Any hobbies? It seemed silly to even wonder about—but it was also, in a funny way, why he seemed cool.

Anyway, I guess Ms. Packer had told Mr. Hendricks I'd been freaking out about climate stuff, because in class the very next day, he announced the Belmont River Project.

"This is always the highlight of my year," he said. "I've done this project with many of your older siblings, and I bet they'll tell you it was a highlight of their year as well. We'll be studying the river for a few weeks, really getting our feet wet. I mean that literally *and* figuratively." He grinned. "We're lucky this year to have all the supplies we need, including some new high-tech ones I'm very excited about—probes and tablets to help us collect data. But I'm asking each of you to bring your own rubber boots on Monday. Waders if possible, but any rubber boots that go up above the ankle. See me privately if that's an issue."

Riley frowned as she took notes. She lived with her mom, who wore fancy shoes and wasn't a fishing sort of person. So I guessed they didn't have stinky old rubber boots in their garage the way we did.

Kenji raised his hand. He'd only been at school for a few days, but he wasn't the least bit shy. "What exactly will we be doing?" he asked.

"Oh, lots of things," Mr. Hendricks said cheerfully. "Taking samples, running tests, charting our results. Comparing our findings to previous years."

"Ooh, fuuunnn," said Tabitha. She rolled her eyes at Kenji, who looked down at his desk.

"It is, Tabitha, I promise you." Mr. Hendricks poked the bridge of his glasses. "But it's more than that. This is a long-term study of the river's health, and we submit our data to the town, so our work has real-world significance. And now let me ask you guys: If you wanted to know if a body of water was healthy, what would you look for?"

"Fish," Xavier Hogan said. It was the sort of automatic, no-thinking comment he gave to everything.

One of the reasons I liked Mr. Hendricks: he had a way of rescuing answers, making people sound smarter than they were. "Yes, Xavier, the presence of fish gives us great information about water quality. Although actually we'll be focusing on *other* wildlife in the river, tiny creatures called macroinvertebrates—macros for short. More ideas?"

"If the water looks clear," Riley said. "Not muddy or cloudy."

"We call that cloudiness 'turbidity,'" Mr. Hendricks said. "And it's one of the tests we'll be doing. Good thinking, Riley."

She beamed. Riley aced every test in every class, and teachers' opinions meant a lot to her.

Archer raised his hand. "If the water is moving the way it should. If it's fast or slow. And also if it's too low or too high."

Mr. Hendricks nodded. "Right. Those are all important physical measures. Other thoughts?"

"Bad smells," Xavier said.

A couple of people laughed. Like "bad smells" was even funny.

Mr. Hendricks stayed serious. "Such as?"

"Archer's farts."

"Shut up, moron," Archer told Xavier.

"Hey, folks, none of *that*," called out Ms. Alcindor from the back of the room. She was Mr. Hendricks's teaching assistant, and she had the kind of voice that made kids shut up right away.

Mr. Hendricks gave her a quick nod and continued. "Smell and taste are both useful tools, although we won't be tasting river water. Got that? *No tasting.* But let me ask again: What sorts of smells *should* we be noting?"

"*Dead* fish?" Tabitha guessed. She made a face.

"Chemicals?" Riley said.

Kenji turned to face her. "Okay, but what do you mean? Because *everything* is made up of chemicals. Including people."

Riley blinked a few times, like she had dust on her eyelashes. "I mean unnatural things that pollute the water."

"Yeah, but there are *natural* things that pollute water too, like soil from farms. And plenty of chemicals don't even *have* a smell. Anyhow, just because a chemical is unnatural doesn't mean it's evil."

The way he was saying this made me think he was quoting someone. I felt my face heating and my Ziggy scab itching.

"That's just stupid," I blurted.

"Excuse me, Haven," Mr. Hendricks said. He looked surprised. "You know that's not a word we use here. And I think Kenji is making a fair point. Because medicines are unnatural chemicals that are highly useful, right? And viruses are natural, but potentially dangerous. So just because something is *natural* doesn't mean it's *good*."

"Okay, sorry," I said. "But Kenji, the other day you were saying we should know about the Great Barrier Reef, right? So I looked it up. And the coral is dying for a lot of reasons, including pesticides, which are *unnatural* chemicals that definitely *don't* belong in the water." I was speaking so fast I needed to gulp a breath. "Although the biggest problem is climate change making the water warmer. And there's nothing natural about that!"

Kenji tossed his hair. I could guess what he was thinking: *Just a few days ago you admitted you didn't even know about the Great Barrier Reef. And now all of a sudden you're some kind of expert?*

Well, if you care about the reef, you should care about FACTS, I answered him in my head. *You should care about science!*

Across the room Riley frowned.

But Mr. Hendricks was smiling. "Well, I see someone's been doing research," he said, looking right at me.

CRUSH

A t lunch after science it was just Riley and me at the table. Most days I brought something veggie from home. But on Fridays they usually had my favorite, mac 'n' cheese, and for a minute I just focused on the warm, comforting gooeyness.

Then I mentioned that my dad had a bunch of old boots he used for fishing. In case she needed a pair for this river thing, I added.

"Really?" she said immediately. "Because I think I might."

"Sure. They're a little gross, but they're waders, and

definitely better than muddy feet. Anyhow, that's what I'm using, so we'll be twins." I grinned. "I'll drop them off at your house tomorrow."

Instead of thanking me, Riley poked the pepperoni on her pizza. Poke, poke, poke, like for an entire minute.

"Is something wrong?" I asked.

She looked up. "Haven, can I say something? I thought you were kind of rude to Kenji."

"What? When?"

"Just now in science."

I stared. "You mean because I disagreed with him? So did you."

"Yes, but I didn't *embarrass* him."

"How did I embarrass him?"

"You know. The way you gave that big speech. About the Great Barrier Reef, and pollution, and all that."

I put down my fork. "Riley, I disagreed with him because he was wrong! Sticking up for chemicals in the water—"

"Kenji wasn't *sticking up for chemicals.* And that's not the point."

"What *is* the point? That he's cute?" My throat felt tight. "So if he's ugly, or a girl, I can disagree with him, but not if you and Em have a crush?"

"Who says I do? Anyhow, that's not fair!"

"*What's* not fair?" Em slid into the empty bench. "What did Haven do?"

"Nothing," I said.

"Nothing," Riley muttered.

And I was grateful for that, even though Riley barely talked to me the whole rest of lunch.

THE BENCH

The next morning, Mom said she'd drive me over to Riley's house to drop off the boots. It was nine fifteen, too early to ring someone's doorbell on a Saturday, so I decided to just leave the boots on the front porch.

But Riley's mom must have spotted me through the window because she opened the door right away.

"Is Ri with you?" she asked, looking past me at the car.

"What? No," I said. "Why would she be?"

"Oh, I thought you were driving her home from Em's sleepover. I have to leave now for work; I guess she'll be getting a lift from Em's mom?"

"Yeah, probably," I said. "I mean, I'm pretty sure she is. Yes."

Riley's mom threw me a funny look, like all of a sudden she could tell I was faking.

"Well, I told Riley I'd bring over some boots for science class, so here they are, bye!" I hurried back to the car before Riley's mom could say anything else.

"Everything okay?" Mom asked as I strapped on my seat belt.

"Yep, fine," I said, avoiding her eyes. I tried to keep my voice cool even though my brain was on fire. *Riley was at Em's house? For a sleepover? Which they both kept secret from me?*

Mom rolled down the windows, then drove us to our favorite bakery—Dough Re Mi—where we bought a still-warm loaf of semolina bread and some fresh-baked muffins. It was a sunny morning with a soft breeze, the kind of weather that made you think that everything was normal, the planet was healthy, all the seasons were happening the way they should.

Mom suggested eating our muffins on one of the benches over by the new baseball field in the center of town. We picked a bench beside a young-looking, skinny dogwood tree, near a bunch of daffodils. Mom handed me the bag of muffins; I took the one on top, wet with blueberries. For a couple of minutes we sat there in the shade, not talking, just eating our muffins, as some kids in Little League uniforms took the field.

This is nice, I told myself. *Try not to think about the sleepover party. Which you weren't invited to. And which no one even told you about.*

Although maybe that's being "too sensitive."

All of a sudden Mom turned to me. "Okay if we talk, sweet potato?"

Uh-oh, I thought. Had she heard what Riley's mom said about the sleepover? If she had, she'd want to know why I wasn't invited. And then, the way moms worked, she'd probably call Riley's mom to talk about it, and make the whole thing even worse.

I picked off a too-big blueberry from the top of my muffin and popped it into my mouth. "Sure," I said, trying to sound casual. "What's up?"

"Well, two things, actually. The first is that I wanted to ask you to try a little harder to get along with your brother. Dad's under a lot of stress at work these days, and all the squabbling between you two is really not helping."

Oh. That.

"Why is Dad under stress?" I asked.

"Well, his job's kind of rough these days. Mostly it's his new boss."

This surprised me, because I hadn't even realized Dad had a new boss.

"Sorry, Mom," I said. "I'll try to ignore Carter. Try *harder*, I mean. But you're telling him too, right?"

"Of course I am." Her eyebrows knitted. "Haven, I'm not saying the fighting is your fault. I know your brother baits you, but you don't *always* have to respond. Especially at the supper table, okay?"

Don't overreact; don't be too sensitive.

"Okay." I broke off some muffin top. "What's the other thing?"

"Sweetheart, your fingernails. They look really sore. Is there a reason you're biting them so much?"

The planet is dying. Animals are in danger.

Nothing I do makes any difference.

My friends are all acting weird.

I don't know.

Everything.

"Not really," I said. "Mostly it's just a habit."

"Well, I'm afraid you'll get an infection."

"I won't, I swear! Anyhow, I wash my hands all the time."

"Yes, but germs are sneaky." Mom looked at me sideways. "Do you remember when you were four and you had chicken pox? I put socks on your hands to keep you from scratching. Maybe we should do that again."

"Mom, are you joking? *Seriously?* You want me to go to school wearing *socks* on my—"

"Calm down, Hay. Yes, of course I'm joking." She reached over to brush some hair out of my eyes. "But there *are* other things we can try. I've been reading about a kind of bracelet that vibrates if you bite your nails. Also there's a special kind of bitter-tasting polish."

Ugh, really? It just seemed wrong and unfair to make me taste bitter stuff on purpose, almost like a punishment for being nervous. Plus I hardly ever wore jewelry, so if I showed up at school with a vibrating bracelet, I'd have to explain it to everyone. *Oh, this? I can't control myself, so I need a zapper. . . .* I could already imagine Em's reaction.

Although thinking of Em made me remember something.

I reminded Mom about the River Project. I'd be dunking my hands in the water to take samples, I explained, which would probably mess up the vibrating bracelet. And maybe nail polish would come off in the river.

"Anyhow," I added quickly, "I think I want to try something else—wearing a rubber band on my wrist. Or a ponytail holder. Which I could snap if I ever feel like biting."

Mom raised her eyebrows. "Hmm. Well, I guess it's worth a try. How long is this River Project?"

HAVEN JACOBS SAVES THE PLANET

"I'm not sure," I said. "I think Mr. Hendricks said around two weeks?"

"All right. I seriously doubt that nail polish comes off so easily, but we'll hold off for now. Do you have enough ponytail holders?"

I nodded.

"Okay, good. Just promise you'll try *extra* hard to keep your hands out of your mouth, *especially* if you're touching that dirty river water."

I promised. But I couldn't help thinking: *Penguins and dolphins and koalas are in danger. People too. The whole Planet Earth! Who cares about my fingernails?*

And then, to change the subject, I said how pretty the new baseball field looked, and how nice these benches were. "Although why do they need all those signs?" I added.

Mom picked a walnut off her muffin. "What signs?"

I pointed to the small brass plaques nailed to each bench: COURTESY OF GEMBA INDUSTRIES.

"Well, you know Gemba's done so much for this town," Mom said. "Not just reopening the factory. Also fixing up this field, and the scoreboard. And these benches, and the community vegetable garden—"

"Okay, but why do they need their name all over everything? Including baseball uniforms." I pointed to a girl standing a few feet away from us. Above her number (fifteen) it said GEMBA in red letters.

Mom took a last bite of muffin. "Yeah, it's a bit much. Although it's thanks to Gemba that we even have a Little League."

"Should we also thank them for our muffins? Maybe we could spell out Gemba in blueberries and walnuts."

"Oh, Haven," Mom said, smiling. "But you know, without Gemba, this town would be in bad trouble. Dad's not the only one who'd lose his job; so would a lot of people. And of course I'd lose students at my preschool."

"You would?"

She brushed some muffin crumbs off her lap. "Sure. If there are no jobs, people don't need day care, right? And even if they need it, they can't afford it. So my feeling is, if Gemba wants to stick their name on everything, I'm good with that."

Well, at least they can't stick their name on the grass, I told myself. *Or on the dogwood tree. Or on the daffodils.*

Or on the river.

SLEEPOVER

When we got home, Riley was sitting on our front steps in her soccer uniform.

"Haven, can we please talk really fast?" she asked. "I have a game at noon, and I told my mom I'd be home in like fifteen minutes."

"Uh, sure," I said.

As we climbed the stairs to my room, I slid the ponytail holder off my hair and onto my wrist. Just in case.

"Okay," Riley said the second I shut my door. "First is that I'm really, really sorry for what I said at lunch yesterday. I shouldn't have blamed you for arguing with Kenji in science. You're right—I think I *may* have a crush. *Possibly.* But that doesn't mean you can't tell him when he's wrong about something. Also, I think it's extremely cool that you know all that stuff. And did research."

"Well, thanks," I said, smiling a little. "But I wouldn't call it research. Just some articles I read online."

"That's definitely research." Her eyes were huge. "You're not mad at me?"

I shook my head.

"Good. I was worried."

She used the past tense, but she still looks worried, I thought.

"There's something else," she said.

What was this—Dump on Haven Day? Suddenly my legs felt like spaghetti; I sat on my bed.

"Go ahead," I said, fingering the ponytail holder.

"Okay. So. Em had this sleepover last night. She invited Tabitha and also me."

"Yeah, I know."

"You *do*?"

"Your mom told me. When I went to drop off the boots this morning."

"Oh. Anyway, I thought, well, if Em's inviting me, she's definitely inviting Haven, because she knows we're best friends, right? But then it was suppertime, and you still hadn't shown up. So I asked Em when you were coming."

"Never, because I wasn't invited." I hugged my knees. "Did she say why not?"

"Yeah, because you're a vegetarian and her mom was making beef chili."

"What? Omigod, Riley, that's the dumbest —"

"Right?"

"Because seriously, who cares about chili?"

"I know! You could have brought your own food."

"Yeah, or Em's mom could have made something without meat. So obviously it *wasn't* just about the chili."

Riley nodded. I waited for her to keep talking, but she stayed quiet.

I ran my pointer finger over the ponytail holder. "So what did you tell her?"

"Well, nothing," Riley said. "I mean, it was Em's house, right? She can invite anyone she wants. Or *not* invite. But after that I just went home because I didn't feel right about leaving you out."

But that's not the truth, Riley. Because when I dropped off the boots this morning, your mom told me you weren't home yet.

Should I say something? And risk losing my best friend? Basically my only friend these days?

Maybe not.

"Thanks." My throat felt like sandpaper. "Did you tell Em why you were leaving?"

"Haven, Em's always really nice to *me*. So I didn't want to start a whole big thing in front of Tabitha. And also Em's family."

Was Riley avoiding my eyes? I swallowed hard. "So you just left her house?"

"I said I had cramps, and then her mom drove me home."

"Oh. Okay."

"Anyway." Riley twisted her hands. "I wasn't sure if I should even tell you, because I knew it would hurt your feelings. But I *hate* keeping secrets from you, Haven. And I thought you'd want to know the truth."

Really? Because it sounds like you're lying to me right now.

I snapped the ponytail holder once. Twice. Harder the second time.

Then I got up. We hugged.

At the door, just as she was leaving my bedroom, Riley turned to me. "Maybe there's a way to tell Em how you feel about being left out. I mean, a way that won't start a big fight."

"Riley, you think she'd even listen? Because she acts like everything I say is a joke!"

"Well, maybe there's a way of telling her that isn't . . . I don't know, *telling* her."

"Yeah, maybe," I said, even though I had no idea what Riley meant.

And I couldn't help thinking that if things were the opposite—if Riley was the one not invited—I wouldn't lie to her about it. I would protest to Em, and also leave as soon as I could. Because sometimes standing up was what really mattered.

THE RIVER PROJECT

The Belmont River ran through the center of town, narrowing to a stream over by the library. When we were little, Archer and I sometimes played in this stream, skimming stones and searching for "buried treasure," like we thought the *Titanic* had sunk there or something. I'd been to the library a zillion times since we started middle school, but lately I hadn't paid attention to the stream; it was sort of like a playground I'd outgrown.

But at the start of class on Monday, Mr. Hendricks told us to put on our boots and grab a clipboard, because that's where we were going. Before we officially started the River

Project, he said, he wanted to show us our stations, explain the equipment and the procedures.

Then he announced river teams.

Some teachers like Ms. Packer paid attention to friendships and enemy-ships, but Mr. Hendricks didn't care about stuff like that. Whenever he assigned us lab partners or teams, they seemed totally random, or based on things like alphabetical order. So it was kind of a shock when he said I was on Team Four— with Riley, Archer, and Kenji.

Riley, who was my best friend, except I felt weird about the sleepover—how she'd lied about sticking up for me.

Archer, who was still my friend, technically, but was definitely avoiding me at school.

And Kenji, who wasn't my friend, and who made me nervous. There was just something about him, and it wasn't only the cuteness or even the way he stuck up for chemicals. Although the truth was that both those things—the cuteness and the chemicals—made me feel squirmy in a way I couldn't explain.

But immediately I yelled at myself. Kirima Ansong wouldn't care about sleepovers, or friendship weirdness, or the way some boy looked, or what he'd said in class. I needed to focus on the River Project—which, like Ms. Packer said, could possibly help somehow. And, according to Mr. Hendricks, had *real-world significance*—even if I didn't know what that meant.

As soon as we all had on boots and jackets, we left the building, following Mr. Hendricks to a spot behind the library parking lot where the stream curved like a sharp elbow.

"Everyone will get the chance to do everything," he announced. "But we have a limited amount of equipment, so we'll need to take turns."

He explained that some teams would start with the physical testing, which was basically taking measurements of the river. Other teams would do chemical testing, measuring stuff like oxygen levels and acidity. The rest of us would do biological testing, checking for wildlife. And then we'd switch.

"But today's just about exploring," Mr. Hendricks added. "Wade in the water, turn over rocks, take notes on your clipboards. You can use your phones to take photos— but word of warning, if your phone gets wet, that's on you. Excuse me."

He hurried off to stop Zeb Waller from shoving Ishaan into the water.

About ten feet away Ms. Alcindor was talking to Team Five—Xavier, Tabitha, Brenna Kapoor, and Shane Callaghan. Shane was a kid who never did any homework, never knew any answers, and even fell asleep sometimes in class. Brenna was obsessed with music; she hardly ever talked about anything else. Xavier and Tabitha were . . . Xavier and Tabitha. My team was awkward, for a bunch of different reasons, but at least everyone was serious about science.

I stepped into the stream. It surprised me how suddenly the water was up to my knees. So I was grateful for Dad's high boots, even if they smelled like old fish.

"Okay, now what?" Archer asked from the bank. His boots just reached the top of his ankles, and I could tell he wasn't thrilled about wading.

"We observe," I said.

"Observe *what*?" Riley said. She swished her hand in the stream. "It's just water. And rocks!"

"Rocks are awesome," Kenji told her as he waded into the water. "Have you ever gone trout fishing?"

"Me? Nope."

"I have," I said. "What *about* rocks?"

"Well, if you've been trout fishing, you should know." Kenji kicked the water. "Fish love rocks; that's where you find them. Also other creatures."

"That's right, Kenji," Mr. Hendricks called out. I blushed, because I hadn't realized he could hear our conversation, with Kenji acting so superior. *You should know.* Why did he always talk to me like that?

"The rocky spots are called riffles," Mr. Hendricks said as he took off his Phillies cap to wipe his forehead. "When water churns over the rocks, oxygen gets dissolved in the water. And you know who needs oxygen?"

"Fish," Xavier called out.

"Remember, Xavier, I said we probably wouldn't see fish," Mr. Hendricks said.

"Bugs, right?" Archer said. "I hate bugs."

"I like *some* bugs, but not mosquitoes," Riley said. "Or spiders. Or stinkbugs."

"In Indonesia stinkbugs smell really bad," Kenji said. "Worse than here. Also they have lynx spiders with fangs. And another kind of spider that jumps."

"Can we please not talk about this?" Archer begged.

Riley was giggling. "Thanks for telling us, Kenji. Now I'm never going to Indonesia."

"All right, folks," Mr. Hendricks said evenly. "Let's stay focused on Belmont wildlife, please. Remember, we'll be looking for macros."

"Won't we need microscopes?" Archer asked.

"Actually, no—macros are tiny but visible. I'll give you magnifying glasses if you need them, and also charts to help with identification."

"Hey, Mr. Hendricks," Xavier shouted, even though Mr. Hendricks was standing like three feet away from him.

"What you said before—if we splash, that means we're adding oxygen to the water?"

"Correct," Mr. Hendricks said. "But please don't splash your teammates."

So of course Xavier started kicking water all over Tabitha and Brenna.

"Omigod, Xavier, you're *such a jerk*," Tabitha squealed, while Brenna put her hands on her hips and shouted, "Hey, stop! You're getting me all wet!"

"Enough, Xavier," Mr. Hendricks said. His voice was stern, but his face looked the same as always—alert, calm, like nothing could surprise or bother him. "All right, now, everybody. Gather round, and let's talk about tools and equipment."

We jumped back onto the bank. Mr. Hendricks started explaining what we'd be using for all the testing. Low-tech stuff like nets, magnifying glasses, and thermometers. High-tech stuff like probes, which we'd stick in the water, and tablets, which would give us readouts.

"We need to treat all these things very carefully," he said, "but especially the probes and tablets. We have only a few, and they'd be too expensive to replace. But we're so grateful for this generous donation by Gemba."

I looked up. *This generous donation by Gemba.* The base-ball field and the benches and the community vegetable garden . . . and also the fancy equipment we were using for the River Project?

Of course I couldn't resent Gemba for donating cool science stuff. How could I? How could any of us? But. Why was everything in this town suddenly *thanks to Gemba*? They'd only been in Belmont for about a year, and it was like they'd tattooed their name on our town forever. There was just something wrong about it, although I couldn't say exactly what it was.

And then a very strange thing happened: Mr. Hendricks lifted his baseball cap and smiled. Right at Kenji.

Wait, what? What does Kenji have to do with Gemba?

And why is Kenji smiling back like that?

I tried to catch Riley's eye, but she was staring at Kenji. Again.

FROGS

That night, as I ate a pepper-and-onion omelet I made for my own supper, I asked Dad about Gemba. Specifically, about his new boss.

"My boss? What about him?" Dad took a big bite of hamburger.

"What do you know about him?" I asked. I turned my head so I didn't have to see the red hamburger juice dripping onto his plate. "Does he have a kid?"

Mom blew on a steamy forkful of baked potato. "Why are you asking, Hay?"

"Just wondering. There's a new boy in my class. And

when we started the River Project today—well, not *started* it, just kind of got ready for it—Mr. Hendricks thanked Gemba for some fancy equipment. But he said it right to this kid."

"Well, I guess it's possible my boss has a son your age," Dad said. "We don't talk very much, and when we do, it's not about family." His forehead puckered.

"But how nice of Gemba to donate to your science class, Haven." Mom gave me a look like *I told you Dad's boss was stressing him out, so let's change the subject, okay?*

But I wasn't finished. "Yeah, Mr. Hendricks said the stuff was really expensive." I turned to Dad, away from Mom's eye message. "So what's your boss's name?"

"Mike Stillman," he said.

Kenji's dad. It has to be!

No wonder Kenji acts stuck-up. Like he's in charge of everyone. Because Gemba is in charge of this whole town!

"So how was the river?" Carter was asking me. "You catch any frogs?"

I shook my head. "There weren't any."

"Sure there were." My brother grinned. "When we did that project, there were *tons* of frogs jumping all over the place! Me and Gavin even caught a few. One little guy we stuck in Ashlyn Russo's backpack."

"That's horrible," I said. "You freed it afterward, right?"

"Obviously." My brother snorted. I had a feeling he was about to call me "Lentil" or something, but he didn't—maybe so we wouldn't be *squabbling at the dinner table*.

"Yeah, Haven, I bet the frogs were just hiding from you," Carter added. "But trust me, the river's full of them. Next time you're over there, you'll see."

"Yeah, maybe," I said.

After dinner I couldn't stop thinking about what Carter had said: how when he'd done the River Project two years ago, the water was full of frogs. I mean, if that was true, I should have spotted one, right? Or at least heard a *ribbit* or something.

That night I researched *Where are the frogs?*

Big mistake.

Frog population in decline on every continent—

Losing about 20 percent of frogs every year—

Causes include disease, pollution, habitat destruction, climate change—

Like honeybees, frogs are portents of environmental collapse—

I chewed my thumbnail until my skin started to throb. Then I wrapped my thumb in two tight Band-Aids and shoved my hands under my pillow.

After that my brain tornadoed. And even though Ziggy cuddled next to me, breathing fish breath all over my face, I couldn't sleep.

It was like I could hear Kirima Ansong's voice in my head, loud and clear: *The planet is melting, disappearing, in danger. Maybe one day we'll wake up and everything on earth will be gone.*

Penguins and whales, honeybees and frogs . . .

Although now I was thinking mostly about the frogs.

Archer texted me at breakfast: Hey you want to hear about Level 5 in RoboRaptors? I found a secret portal.

But this morning I couldn't answer, couldn't even do an emoji. Instead I texted back: Hey Archer, can I ask you a question? When we were at the river yesterday, did you see any frogs?

Archer: Why?

Me: Just curious. Carter said he saw tons of frogs 2 yrs ago.

Archer: Oh. Well no I didn't, actually.

Me: Neither did I. I think maybe they're all gone because of climate change???

Archer: Oh. Hadn't thought about that. Tbh I don't even like frogs. But if they're endangered . . . that's v scary.

Me: Yeah, it is. ☹

Archer: ALL this climate stuff is v scary tho, right? Can I tell you something? Sometimes when I start to think about it too much I freak out. So I try not to.

Me: Is that why you game so much?

Archer: Not the only reason!!

Me: Shrug

Archer: I mean I just really like to play!! But I guess maybe, IDK. Sometimes.

Me: Okay, but don't you wish we could DO something?? Not just play games.

Archer: Sure. Like what?

Me: No idea. That's the problem.

Archer: Yep.

Pause.

Archer: Okay well see you later Haven.

This conversation didn't make me feel any better. Actually, it made me feel worse, because it meant I hadn't imagined the river's froglessness.

But at least Archer was texting me about a real thing, an important thing, not some dumb game I wasn't even playing.

I chewed my toast, wondering what it meant. If it meant anything at all.

STORM

On Tuesday our class went back to the river. It had stormed all Monday night—a heavy, windy rain that pulled down branches—and now the soggy ground squished under my boots.

The kind of bad rainstorm I used to have nightmares about. The kind that made your bed float away.

Did we always have terrible storms like this? It felt like the answer was no, although it wasn't like I could remember old weather.

Anyway, I made it to the river without too much slipping, thanks to the treads on Dad's old waders. And when we got to our team's station, I was surprised to see how high the water was, how fast it was moving over leaves and branches and rocks and random bits of garbage—newspapers and soda cans, mostly—tossed in by the rainstorm.

"Eww, the river looks like a trash can," Tabitha said. "And it smells kind of funny. Don't you think, Mr. Hendricks?"

Mr. Hendricks seemed excited by everything—the muddy smell, all the extra water, even the floating garbage. "Take note of as much as you can, folks. Next time we come it'll be totally different. That's what I love about the river! It's always changing."

"Hey, Mr. Hendricks," Xavier called out, grinning. "Tabitha says she wants to take a swim!"

"Omigod, I do *not*," Tabitha yelled at him. "That water's disgusting! And so are you, Xavier!"

"*And* let's try to behave like middle schoolers," Mr. Hendricks said. He told our team to start with physical testing—measuring the river's dimensions, using a rubber duck to calculate water speed, taking the water temperature.

The river was six feet wide, ten degrees Celsius. I used my phone to translate the temperature into Fahrenheit: fifty degrees. *Is that normal?* I wondered as I recorded it on my clipboard. I really wanted this project to show something. Mean something. And climate change caused too-warm water—even for streams like this, right?

Maybe the water temperature was bad for frogs. And that was one reason they'd disappeared.

Mr. Hendricks checked our clipboards, although he didn't seem too interested in any of the numbers, even the water temperature.

"Okay, Team Four, you're ready for wildlife identification," he told us. "Wade in the water carefully, please. Macros are delicate, so no stomping."

He showed us how to position the net, swish the water, and pick up stones to remove the macros. We'd also use the net to scoop the macros from the stream bottom, and to scrape them off twigs and branches in the water. All macros would be collected in the basins, where we'd identify them using the charts.

"For macro collection, we work in pairs," Mr. Hendricks said. "Which I'll leave up to you." He hurried off.

Pairs? That we choose ourselves?

Riley, Archer, Kenji, and I eyed each other like we were being forced to do the square-dance unit in PE. As soon as my eyes met Archer's, he looked away.

"I'll work with Haven," Kenji said.

Wait, what? No!

"Oh, okay," Riley said immediately. She turned away from me as she lifted a basin from the stack.

I grabbed her arm. "Let's switch," I murmured. "*You*

pair with Kenji, all right? Or why don't we just pair together?"

"No, Haven, Kenji wants to pair with you," she replied, shrugging. Before I could stop her, she walked over to Archer.

I watched Kenji toss his hair out of his eyes. He was friends with Archer, so it made zero sense that he'd picked me, really. Maybe he knew his dad was the boss of my dad, and he thought he could boss me too.

"Ready?" he asked me.

Instead of answering, I waded into the water.

YELLOW

One thing I had to admit about Kenji: he took science seriously. He didn't fool around or splash like Xavier, or complain about everything, like Tabitha. And he wasn't grossed out by bugs, like Archer.

So even though the two of us barely spoke, we did collect a bunch of macros. Way more than Riley and Archer, who seemed to do nothing but argue (she was holding the net too low, he wasn't scraping enough, blahblahblah).

When Ms. Alcindor noticed that our basin was almost full, she told us it was time to start the identification.

Kenji frowned at our basin. "All right, but how? It just looks like a big blob of mud."

"We have some little paintbrushes to help you separate out the macros, or you can just use your fingers," Ms. Alcindor said. "You'll probably need your magnifying glass, and definitely the identification chart."

I sat on the riverbank. Ms. Alcindor made it sound pretty simple, but to be honest, all these creatures looked the same to me, even with a magnifying glass.

Well, basically the same.

Well, no, not really.

Actually, the more you studied them, the more you saw. Bodies like skinny worms. Black heads, tiny legs, suction pads.

"Okay, I think I can name a few of them," I announced after checking the chart. "That's definitely a midge-fly larva over there. This squiggly one's an aquatic worm. And I'm pretty sure the one in the corner is blackfly larva."

"Huh," Kenji said. "You could be right."

"Actually, I'm sure I *am* right," I said.

We glared at each other.

Then Kenji pointed to the basin, where a brown, slimy-looking macro about an inch long had settled in the corner opposite the blackfly larva.

"What's that one?" he asked. "A leech?"

I squinted at the creature, then at the chart. "Yep. Exactly."

"Gross."

I shrugged. Ever since the trout incident, I'd sort of trained myself not to think that way. "Animals are animals," I said. "It's not a beauty contest; we shouldn't rate them."

Now he grunted. Because, bleh, I'd probably sounded kind of know-it-all-y, like I was Haven Jacobs, Defender of Leeches. And it wasn't like I cared about them, anyway; honestly, I was more focused on the frogs.

Although, why was that? Because frogs were cute?

Why was cuteness always so important?

Animals are animals, I repeated to myself.

The funny thing was that now I was blushing.

"Okay, Team Four, whatcha got?" Mr. Hendricks was behind us now, rubbing his hands together.

"We found these," I said, showing Mr. Hendricks the section of the chart where it said *Group Three Taxa: Pollution-tolerant organisms can be in any quality of water.*

"Interesting," Mr. Hendricks said. He tapped the bridge of his glasses as he stared into our basin. "That's all? No caddis flies? Or mayflies? Or riffle beetles?"

Why was he asking? Had we messed up? Missed macros we should have noticed? Read the chart wrong?

"We didn't see any," Kenji admitted.

"Also no frogs," I added.

Kenji frowned. Maybe he thought this was off topic. But it wasn't!

Mr. Hendricks raised his eyebrows at Ms. Alcindor. Right away I could tell it was one of those wordless grown-up conversations where kids weren't invited. And if you asked what it was about, they wouldn't tell you, probably.

But I had to know. "Is something wrong?"

Mr. Hendricks didn't answer. "What about you?" he asked Archer and Riley. "Find any of these?" He pointed to the chart section titled *Group One Taxa: Pollution-sensitive organisms found in good quality water.*

"No," Archer said. "Although we're not finished."

"Because *someone* won't touch anything wormy," Riley said.

"I'm touching them! I'm just trying to be careful."

"Ha, right," Riley said. "Careful to let *me* do all the work."

Mr. Hendricks turned around to talk in private to Ms. Alcindor, who nodded, frowning. What was going on? From the look on Kenji's face, I could tell he wondered too.

Now Mr. Hendricks faced us again. "All right, Team Four. We'll follow up with more wildlife observation next time. For now, why don't you folks switch to chemical testing."

Right away Ms. Alcindor handed us strips of litmus paper, which she told us to hold in the water for five minutes. Pure water was perfectly neutral, she said, neither acidic nor alkaline—a seven on the pH scale, which went from zero (acid) to fourteen (alkaline). If the water was acidic—registering as anything less than seven—the paper would turn gray or yellow or orange. Alkaline water turned the paper blue or purple, and would be a higher number, all the way up to fourteen.

"Just get the paper wet? That's all we do?" Riley asked.

"Yep," Ms. Alcindor said. "Easy-peasy."

"This is basically kindergarten," Riley muttered to me. "Colors and numbers. Don't you think, Haven?"

But I didn't feel like chatting. I squatted at the edge of the river, watching the water race across my litmus paper.

"All right, folks. What color did you get?" Ms. Alcindor called out in her strong, bright voice.

"Yellow," I said.

"Really?"

I showed her my wet strip. "Looks like a five-point-five on the scale. Possibly a five-point-four."

"Huh," she said. "That's definitely acidic. What about you?" she asked Archer.

He shrugged. "Same."

"Hold on, let me get Mr. Hendricks. These strips may

have expired or something." She hurried off. We watched her talk to Mr. Hendricks, who'd been checking Xavier's clipboard.

Archer's eyes met mine. Was he thinking what I was, that we'd discovered something weird about the water? Just when I thought Archer would say something to me—a normal sentence in public, like he used to—he looked away. And even took a couple of steps over to Riley.

Mr. Hendricks hurried over, followed by Ms. Alcindor. His face looked thoughtful as he dipped a litmus strip in the water.

"I've done this project for the past seven years, and we always get a few quirky findings," he told us, smiling a little. "Usually we get a result of six-point-five, occasionally a six. You folks have hit the jackpot."

He took the strip out of the water. We could all see: it was yellow, just like ours. Meaning acid in the water.

"That's odd," he said. And now he wasn't smiling.

QUESTIONS

As our class sloshed back over to school, I ran up to the front so I could talk to Mr. Hendricks.

"What did that mean?" I asked him, panting a little. "The litmus paper turning yellow. That's not normal for river water, right?"

"Well, I haven't seen it before," he admitted.

"So if it's yellow, that means the river is full of ... *acid*?"

Mr. Hendricks took a second to answer. "I'm not sure what it means, exactly. But you know, with a big rainstorm, all sorts of stuff can blow into the water. And rainwater itself is slightly acidic, so that can definitely skew our results. We'll need to repeat the litmus test in other weather conditions. All the tests, in fact."

"Okay, but what about the wildlife? We only found macros that are 'pollution tolerant.' So if all the *other* macros disappeared, the pollution-*sensitive* ones, that's because the river is polluted, right?"

"You're thinking well about this, Haven," he said quietly. "But let's not jump to any conclusions, okay? We do this study over a period of time, because scientists never rely on just one sample, or just one test."

"But it wasn't just one test! Archer and Riley did it too, and so did you and Ms. Alcindor!"

"I mean we need to repeat the test on different days. Remember what I said about the river—it's always different, always changing. That's what's so fascinating about it."

Then Tabitha and Xavier came over to complain about each other.

So I didn't get to ask Mr. Hendricks the other question that was on my mind, blinking in neon lights since last night:

Where are all the frogs?

At lunch Em wouldn't stop talking about some Netflix series she was watching, about some guy who didn't know he was actually an android. Riley was watching it too; I'd never even heard of it before, so all I could do was eat my hummus.

After lunch was social studies. Ms. Packer always greeted everyone in the hallway, so it was impossible to avoid her as you walked into the classroom.

"Haven, how's that missing homework coming along?" she asked.

"It's okay," I said.

"Really?" She cocked her head. "You know, I've been thinking. Instead of writing up all that work, you could do an oral report, if you'd rather."

"You mean in front of the whole class?" If there was anything I hated most about school, it was oral reports. The second I stood up in front of a group, my head buzzed, my knees wobbled, and my mouth dried up. I knew Kirima Ansong forced herself to give speeches. But Kirima was a superhero, and I wasn't.

"No thank you," I said quickly. "I'll just write the homework."

"All right, well, I'd like to see it by tomorrow," Ms. Packer said. It was a deadline; she didn't seem angry, though.

A couple of minutes later she was telling the class about the California Gold Rush, the way miners would swirl some river gravel in a pan of water, watching for gold dust to settle to the bottom.

But rivers aren't only about gold, I thought.

Because even with all the questions swirling in my brain, the stuff I didn't understand and knew I didn't understand, I was definitely sure about that.

After school I sat in the kitchen eating a bowl of Lucky Charms and chocolate milk, thinking about the weirdness at the river today: the test results, Mr. Hendricks's reaction, and also how Kenji had wanted to pair with me. I mean, Kenji didn't even seem to like me as a friend, much less as a crush. And I definitely didn't like him back. But I couldn't help wondering: What would Kenji say if I tried to talk to him about all the Gemba signs in town? He'd probably do a commercial for his dad's business, tell me how great Gemba was to donate so much stuff to boring little Belmont. Including the fancy science equipment our class was using at the river.

And if he said that, how would I respond—if I responded at all? I hadn't told Archer how I felt about him avoiding me at school. I hadn't told Em how I felt about the sleepover business. I hadn't even told Riley how I felt about her telling me she'd left Em's sleepover when she actually hadn't. It was strange: I squabbled with Carter all the time, but sometimes when it came to my friends, I was kind of a wimp, wasn't I?

Ugh. I'd always thought of myself as a doer, a fighter.

Someone who solved problems. But maybe that wasn't true. Or maybe it used to be true, but wasn't anymore. Not since I started seventh grade and my friends got weird.

And all the frogs disappeared, and the glaciers started melting under our feet.

AVOCADO

fter everything that had happened at the river, I couldn't think about starting Ms. Packer's boring homework. I needed something to do with my hands—instead of biting my nails or snapping my wrist.

So after I finished my snack, I decided to try this recipe I'd been saving: chocolate-chip cookies made with avocado instead of butter. They'd be either disgusting or delicious, I couldn't tell which. But at least baking would distract me from all my friend problems. Plus it would keep me off the internet, so I wouldn't be able to research *missing frogs* or *acid in the water*, or *pollution-tolerant*

macros, or anything else that would freak me out about the River Project.

I was just taking the first batch out of the oven when Carter walked into the kitchen, sweaty and red-faced from basketball.

"*Coo*-kies," he shouted in a Cookie Monster voice as he grabbed one and stuffed it into his mouth.

"Careful, they're still hot." I watched him chew. "What do you think?"

"Not bad. Chewy. It tastes a little different." He picked up another cookie. "Why is it a funny color?"

"I used avocado. Don't say anything."

"I wasn't going to." He popped it into his mouth. "Anyhow, they still count as chocolate-chip cookies, so. Thanks."

I was still full from the Lucky Charms, but of course I had to sample one. I chose a small bumpy-looking cookie while Carter poured himself a glass of milk.

He's right, I thought. *Different, but not bad. On the cookie scale, probably a six.*

And watching my brother eating the cookies I'd made—not just eating but actually admitting he *liked* them—made me wonder if we could have a real conversation.

"Carter, can I ask you a question?" I said.

"I don't know, can you?" He grinned; his teeth were smeared with chocolate.

I handed him a napkin. "Remember the testing you did for the River Project? The litmus-paper stuff, and the wild-life observation?"

"Nah. That was two years ago."

"I know. But if you got some funny results, you'd remember, right?"

"Maybe. Depends what you mean by funny."

I explained about the acid in the river water. And the fact that the only macros we found were pollution toler-ant. "All the pollution-*sensitive* macros were missing," I added.

"Huh," he said. "You mean like their feelings were hurt, Lentil?"

I got up from the table. "All right, forget it."

"Haven, come on, I was only joking—"

"You know what, Carter? I thought you cared about climate stuff. And the planet. And what's happening in Belmont."

"Right, I do!"

"But you care *more* about being a jerk. Never mind!"

I went upstairs to my bedroom and shut the door. Ziggy was sleeping on my bed; the second I plopped down next to him, he started purring.

Ziggy, you're the only good thing, I told him in my head. *Everything else in the world is so messed up. And if I try to talk*

to people about it, they treat it like a joke. Or they want to talk
about video games. Or sleepovers. Or fingernails.

The river is in trouble, the planet is in trouble, the frogs are
missing, and no one is paying attention. Or doing anything to
help! Even Mr. Hendricks—

A knock on my door.

I buried my head in Ziggy's fur.

"Haven? Can I come in?" my brother called.

"No," I said.

"Come on, I have something to show you."

"Just go away, Carter."

"Look, you're right, I *was* being a jerk, and I'm sorry,
okay? I won't call you that name from now on, I swear." He
paused. "Anyhow, I really think you'll want to see this."

"See what?"

"Let me in and I'll show you."

"All right, fine," I said.

Carter opened the door and sat on my bed. I tried not to
inhale his basketball sweat as he handed me a folder.

"What's this?" I asked.

"My notes from when I did the River Project. I can't
believe I kept them all this time. Look." He flipped open
the packet. "See? We did litmus testing over six days, and
we always got a reading of slightly acidic—six-point-five
on the pH scale. So that's gray on the litmus strip, right?

Never yellow. And look at our wildlife observation. We saw a *ton* of these guys."

He pointed to the same identification chart we'd used at the river today. Stone flies, caddis flies, mayflies, riffle beetles.

Group One Taxa: Pollution-sensitive organisms found in good-quality water.

"We didn't see *any* of these macros," I said. "Not a single one."

"Yeah, you told me." My brother's eyes were serious. "It's a little scary."

"It is. And you know what else? No frogs, either."

"That's why I'm showing you this, Haven. I think maybe you're right—something's wrong with the river."

"Carter, I *know* I'm right," I said.

He didn't challenge me, or tease me. He just nodded.

And that should have felt like a win, but it didn't.

CATS AND DOGS

"aven, can I ask a question?" Riley asked.

We were at the river for our second day of testing. Today the weather was the opposite of yesterday—hot and dry, with barely any wind. This time the water looked clear, with no funny smell, although you could still see bits of litter—a plastic bag, a smashed soda can, an empty take-out carton, someone's old sneaker—stuck to some rocks, or floating downstream.

I grabbed a basin and a magnifying glass. "What sort of question?"

"About Archer," Riley said behind her hand. "What's going on? Did you two have a fight or something?"

"No. We're still friends, technically. He texts me all the time."

"Really? Because . . . well, for the last few weeks I haven't seen you talking to each other. I mean, *at all.* When we're in a group, it always feels kind of awkward. And every time I go over to you, he moves away."

I didn't answer.

"Have you asked him what's going on?"

I shrugged. "Riley, I can't just ask him if he won't even talk to me."

"But don't you want to know?"

Did I? To be honest, I wasn't sure. What if he told me something I didn't want to hear? Maybe it was enough just to text. Easier to end a conversation if it got uncomfortable.

"Maybe there's a way to ask that won't seem like asking," Riley said.

It sounded like what she'd said about the sleepover, how maybe I could tell Em how I felt without actually *telling* her. Whatever that meant. "Yeah? Like how?"

"I'm not sure, Haven. But I really think—"

Just then I spotted Kenji walking toward us in that

way he had—shoulders first, like he couldn't wait to get where he was going—so I poked Riley to stop talking.

"Ready?" Kenji asked me, ignoring Riley.

He seemed impatient to get to work. So was I, actually.

We started with the physical testing. The water was lower today, not as fast as yesterday, but so what? To be honest, I wasn't super focused on these measurements. I cared much more about the litmus testing; so did Kenji, apparently, because he seemed upset when our test strip came up yellow again.

"So if there's acid in the water today, it's not from the rain," he said.

"Yeah, that's what I'm worried about," I admitted.

He peeked at me from under his bangs. "You're worried?"

"Well, sure. Aren't you?"

He frowned. Was he frowning at me, or at the river?

When we did the wildlife observation, he got even quieter. Again, all we found were leeches, aquatic worms, and blackfly larvae. Macros that were fine with whatever was in the water—acid, old sneakers, whatever.

"And no frogs again," I announced.

Kenji looked up at me. "Why do you keep saying that, Haven? Do you like frogs that much?"

"Not really. I mean, I *like* them, but." My cheeks were

hot, but for some reason I kept talking. "Actually, my favorite animal is cats."

"Seriously?"

"Why, you *don't* like cats?"

He shrugged. "They're not very friendly."

"Sure they are! They're just—" I was about to say *sensitive*, but I stopped myself. "You just have to get to know them. And respect their feelings."

"Maybe. Anyhow, I like dogs best."

"You have one?"

"Can't."

"How come?"

"Because we travel all the time. My dad says it wouldn't be fair. To the dog, I mean."

"Okay, but what about to *you*?"

The way Kenji flinched, I could tell I'd surprised him with that question. And right away I was sorry I'd asked it.

"My dad doesn't think like that," he said quietly.

"Oh, okay. Sorry."

Awkward silence. So after a few seconds I blurted, "Well, I don't know what I'd do without my Ziggy."

"Your *what*?"

"My cat, Ziggy Stardust. My parents named him after a song by David Bowie."

Finally Kenji's face relaxed. He even smiled. "Oh, I know that song."

"You *do*?" Now it was my turn to be surprised. No one my age ever heard of "Ziggy Stardust," so I'd gotten used to explaining my cat's name.

Kenji opened his mouth like he was about to say something else. But just then Riley came over. "Hey, you find any stone flies this time? Or caddis flies?"

"Nope." I showed Riley our basin. "And Carter told me he saw a *ton* two years ago. He even showed me his notes."

"Who's Carter?" Kenji asked.

"My brother," I said. "He's in ninth grade. When he did this River Project with Mr. Hendricks, he also saw frogs. That's how I know they're missing."

Kenji said a strange thing then. "You're a little sister, Haven? You don't seem like one."

"What does that mean?"

"Nothing."

Riley threw me a look I couldn't decipher. Then she walked over to Archer, who was definitely hanging back, writing something on his clipboard. Avoiding my eyes again.

Right then I had this feeling: *I don't understand anything.* Not just what was happening with the river, but with people, too. I never used to feel this way, but now, all of a

sudden, everything felt like a giant mystery, with no identification chart. No test strips, no fancy equipment to help
make sense of what I was seeing.

I was on my own, in the dark. And all around me, it
felt like things were changing, shifting, too fast for me to
keep up.

PROBE

All right, Team Four." Mr. Hendricks was standing behind Kenji, rubbing his hands. "Whatcha got?"

"Same as yesterday," Kenji said. "Acidic water, and only pollution-tolerant macros. So this isn't about the rainstorm, right?"

"Maybe, maybe not," Mr. Hendricks said. He rubbed his chin like he had an invisible beard. "A big storm can have a lasting impact."

"But the water level is so much lower today," I said. "So doesn't that mean most of the rainwater is downstream by now?"

"Possibly, but we need a more complete picture. Has Team Four had a turn reading dissolved-oxygen levels? No? Where's the probe?"

Ms. Alcindor came over with a device the size of a phone. First she explained that the amount of dissolved oxygen would tell us how well the river was supporting living things, like macros. Then she showed us—Kenji, Riley, Archer, and me—how to plug in the sensor, where to position it in the river, how to read it.

"Careful with this thing," she told us. "It's delicate and expensive."

Yes, we know. A gift from Gemba, right?

I peeked at Kenji; he was a few feet away, standing with Archer, who was talking to him in a normal way. The way he used to talk to me.

"Okay, who's probing?" Riley asked.

"Me," I said right away. Because I desperately needed something to do with my hands—and anyway, I had the tallest boots.

So while Kenji, Riley, and Archer stayed on the bank, I sloshed through our section of the river, carefully positioning the probe in riffles, near rocks, on the surface, in the bottom. Every time I got a reading, I called it out to Archer, who recorded the number on his clipboard. And then we waited. . . .

After about ten minutes Mr. Hendricks came over to check the clipboard.

"Huh," he said, exhaling slowly. "Yeah, these oxygen levels are definitely low. Lower than we've seen before. And Teams Two and Five had almost the same numbers."

Ms. Alcindor came over to look at the clipboard. She said something to Mr. Hendricks we couldn't hear. He answered. She nodded.

"But what would *cause* low levels of oxygen?" I asked loudly.

"Haven, we shouldn't speculate," Mr. Hendricks said.

"How come?" *A bad answer is better than no answer, right?*

Mr. Hendricks squinted as he held up his hand to shield his eyes from the sun. "Because I think we need more data before we can even ask the right questions. Also, if we can arrange it, I'd like to call an expert to come out with us next time."

"An expert?" Archer said. "Like who?"

"A professor friend from a community college not far away. Her name is Dr. Ada Lopez, and she specializes in stream studies."

"She writes an excellent blog about water quality," Ms. Alcindor added. "I'm sure she'll be a big help."

Okay, I thought. *So this means Mr. Hendricks and Ms.*

Alcindor also have questions. Knowing this should have made me feel better, because all I'd wanted—or all I'd thought I'd wanted—was for some grown-ups to focus on our team's weird results. The fact that our teachers were calling an expert meant they *were* taking our results seriously. But it also meant they were worried.

So of course I worried too. Even more than I'd worried before.

That afternoon we had a sub for math who showed a video about the Egyptian numerical system. It was so boring that I zoned out, chewing my nails, thinking about the river. All the questions I had. The way my team had acted, especially Kenji and Archer.

And suddenly I remembered what I'd promised Mom—how I'd wash my hands after touching the river. Luckily, the sub let me go to the bathroom, where I scrubbed my fingernails with blue liquid soap and freezing water.

Then I locked myself in a stall, took out my phone, and typed *low oxygen in river.* I made sure to skip the random stuff that popped up whenever you did a search, because obviously I needed to read stuff only by actual scientists.

A lot of what I found was super technical, and I didn't understand all the words and numbers. But I got the gist:

Various factors, including dumping of
chemicals—
 Prolonged periods of hot, sunny days
lead to low levels of dissolved oxygen—
 May be a single pollution event or a
continuous source—
 Possibly climate change—

Then I typed *low oxygen in water effect on frogs*:

 Concerns regarding dissolved oxygen
in Earth's bodies of water due to climate
change—
 Estimated that dissolved oxygen will
continue to decrease over the next century—
 Significant impact on the diving
mechanics of frogs—

My stomach cramped, followed by another attack of diarrhea. Bleh.

I washed my hands again, this time for an entire minute, turned off my phone, and went back to math, where the Egyptian numerical system was the only topic you were supposed to worry about.

ARCHER

*A*fter what Riley said to me at the river, I couldn't stop thinking about Archer. All afternoon, I kept trying to remember when things had first gotten weird between us. When I'd first noticed that things had gotten weird.

But it wasn't like one specific day Archer and I had a fight, and a door slammed. It was more like little by little, inch by inch, he'd pulled away from me at school. At first I wasn't even sure it was happening, because he was still texting me about the dumb games he was playing. So maybe I was imagining it, I told myself. And maybe if I said something, demanded an explanation, I'd just push him further away.

Archer was my oldest friend; I'd known him since pre-school. He was also my only friend who was a boy—although I never thought of him as *a boy*, just as a smart, slightly nerdy kid I used to collect rocks with, borrow books from, skateboard with (until I twisted my ankle). And even though it hurt to see him sit with other kids at lunch, and avoid me in homeroom and in the hallways, I told myself that this was just school behavior. And that he was, after all, *a boy*—so probably I understood him less than I thought I did.

Although, in a funny way, Archer texting that he was worried about the frogs—about the planet, too—made me feel closer to him than I had in weeks. So maybe Riley was right: it was time for Archer and me to talk. I mean, not text, but have an *actual conversation*. Face-to-face, just the two of us.

After dismissal I hung out in the school library for about twenty minutes. I figured this would give Archer enough time to get home, and then I'd head over to his house. Where I hadn't been in more than a month, so my heart was banging as I rang the doorbell.

Archer's mom answered the door with a hug and a shout. Everything about her was always big—big hoop earrings, big sweaters, big hugs. Her name was Min; I'd first met her when I was like three, so I'd always called her by her first name, never Ms. Zhang.

"Haven? Oh wow, come in, honey!" she said as she squeezed me. "How have you been? I haven't seen you in ages!"

"I've been fine, thanks." I cleared my throat. "Is Archer here?"

"In his room. But come talk to me first! I made lemonade!" Already she was pouring me a glass. "How's your mom?"

Min was a reporter for the *Belmont Bee*, the daily newspaper for all the local towns. By now I was used to the way she asked questions—smiling, sharing snacks, but also never letting you escape.

I told her about Mom's preschool, and Dad's job at Gemba, and Carter's high school, and then she asked about my cooking (Min liked to cook too). Just when I was afraid she'd switch topics to Archer and me (did she know more than I did? I couldn't tell), her phone rang.

"Oops, gotta take this, Haven," she said. "Important source for a story! Go talk to Archer now, okay?"

As I climbed the steps to Archer's room, I could hear Min's loud voice: "Yes, but that's not good enough! We need a *direct quote!*" Min was cool and fun, but she was a tough reporter; sometimes I wondered what it would be like to have her for a mom.

I had to knock on Archer's door three times before he opened it.

"Oh," he said when he finally did. He was wearing ear-buds; probably he'd been playing one of his dumb games. "Um, hi, Haven."

"Hi. Can I come in? Your mom said I could," I added, immediately realizing how babyish that sounded.

Archer took off his earbuds and moved from the doorway. I followed him inside his room, which smelled like a cross between boy sweat and Doritos.

He sat at his desk. There wasn't another chair, which meant I had to stand. Awkward.

"So what's up?" he asked, his mouth twitching downward at the corners.

"Nothing," I said. "We need a reason to talk?"

He shrugged. "No. You just never come here anymore."

"Yeah, because you never invite me." I made myself take a breath. Two breaths. "Can I ask you a question, Archer? Is something wrong? I mean, did something happen between us?"

"Not really."

"Well, you're definitely avoiding me at school. I'm not the only one who thinks so. Today Riley asked what's going on."

"I just." Archer's face shrank and his voice got small. "Do we have to talk about this?"

"Yeah, we do." Now I crossed my arms, mostly to keep my heart from leaping out of my chest.

"So . . . well, one thing is that I really don't like Em. And she's always hanging around you these days."

"Em? But she's Riley's friend, not mine! I can't help it if she's always there! And why are you taking that out on *me*?"

He stared at his socks. "Okay, so there's this other thing too. But I don't . . ."

"You don't what?"

"I'm not comfortable talking about it."

Sometimes Archer slowed down his speech, so it was like he was choosing his words syllable by syllable. Whenever he did this, I just spoke faster.

"You think *I'm* comfortable?" I said. "Anyhow, you can't say that without saying *why*."

"Haven, you won't like hearing it."

"Say it anyway. A bad answer is better than a blank."

"What?"

"Nothing. Just something my grandpa used to tell me." When Archer didn't respond, I kept going. "But he didn't mean an answer that was hard to hear. He meant like an answer on a test. He wanted me to get points, even when I hadn't studied. So he was saying I should answer every question."

Why was I babbling about this? It was totally off topic.

Archer twisted his hands. "All right, Haven. You really

want to hear the truth? People at school were saying stuff about us. About you."

"About *me*? What kind of stuff?"

"How you looked. How you were my girlfriend. Et cetera."

"*What*? But that's ridiculous!"

"Yeah, well, it got pretty bad. They drew these gross pictures of us and put them in my locker."

I stared at him. "Who did?"

"Xavier and his friends. I think a few eighth graders too."

"Oh."

Gross pictures of us both? Including me?

It felt like I'd been kicked in the stomach.

"You told them to stop?" My voice squeaked.

"Sure, but they kept doing it. Doing it even *more*. Finally I figured the best thing was just to stay away from you at school. Let them think we'd had a fight or something. And it worked, because they stopped bugging me. And the pictures stopped too."

"Huh," I said. "So in other words, you let these jerks wreck our friendship."

Archer's face crinkled up. "Guys in seventh grade aren't supposed to hang out with girls unless they're, you know, *going out*. I got sick of all the teasing, okay? Some days it was like I didn't even want to go to school. And I really thought we could still be friends, you know? Just . . . maybe not like before."

From the catch in his voice, I could hear he was shaky. But I didn't care. "How come you never told me this?"

"Because I knew you'd get upset! You can be really sensitive, Haven. And you never let things go."

"You're saying *my feelings* were the problem? But you just said *you* were sick of the teasing, right? So this was about *your* feelings, Archer, not mine."

He didn't argue.

"And not letting things go is *good* sometimes," I added. "That's why Kirima Ansong is such a hero! And why your mom is a great reporter, right? Because she keeps asking questions."

I waited, but Archer stayed quiet, like he'd already logged out of this conversation. Or maybe he thought if he said something else, he'd start to cry.

And all of a sudden I felt sorry for him. So I flicked my hand. "You know what, Archer? Don't worry about it."

Now a small smile crept across his face. "Seriously, Haven? 'Don't worry'? I don't think I've ever heard you say that before."

THE TRUTH

I stayed only a few more minutes, because Min came upstairs and started bugging Archer about homework and practicing his saxophone for band. To be honest, I was glad for the interruption, because I needed to process what Archer had told me.

The walk back home took about twenty minutes, but it was a warm afternoon with a light breeze, and the air felt good on my face. Belmont could be incredibly pretty this time of year, with daffodils and crocuses and trees flowering in Crayola colors. So again I had this thought: *The season is behaving the way it should. Maybe the planet is actually . . . okay?*

No, I answered myself. *Because you read all those articles, watched all those videos. So you know the truth, Haven.*

The truth.

What was so great about knowing the truth? Why did I care so much about getting answers? Finally I knew the truth about Archer—a big mystery solved at last, yaaaay. Did knowing the truth make me feel any better? I honestly couldn't say it did. In fact, hearing about Xavier's gross pictures, and the way Archer had dealt with them (or hadn't), actually made me feel worse.

I mean, how could I *not* be upset about the pictures? Of *me.*

And why *didn't* Archer fight those kids off? Or even tell me what was going on? Plus, the stuff he said about how I was "sensitive"—he'd made it seem like the whole thing was my fault, when of course it wasn't.

I had no idea what should happen next. Was I supposed to be mad at Archer now, maybe totally stop being his friend? Forgive him and pretend all the avoiding never happened? Wait and see how he acted? Confront Xavier and his obnoxious friends, and risk the whole thing starting over?

I was more confused now than before. It was like knowing the truth about Em's sleepover: all it did was scramble my brain about Riley.

And even learning all that stuff about the planet, and the river: What was the point of knowing the truth about something if you didn't know what to *do* with it?

I used to feel like I could solve problems. That it was babyish *not* to solve problems, to stand still and let your family find you when you got separated at the state fair.

But lately it was like the more lost I was—the more I *knew* how lost I was—the less I could imagine running.

By the time I got home, Mom was in the kitchen, filling a big pot with water from the faucet. "I thought we'd do spaghetti primavera tonight," she was saying. "I'll grate some Parmesan. Can you please help with the veggies?"

"Sure," I said as I put down my backpack. Chopping vegetables—that was something I could do. Something useful and specific.

I could feel Mom's eyes checking my fingernails as I washed my hands at the sink. Had I been biting today? I wasn't sure; the biting happened when I was thinking about other things. But maybe thanks to the ponytail holders I kept around my wrist, my nails were looking better lately, not so pink or raw. And the way Mom didn't comment, I could tell she thought so too.

I carefully dried my hands on a towel, peeled some carrots, and started chopping.

"So," Mom said.

Uh-oh. Here we go. Bitter nail polish, vibrating bracelets.

"You were over at Archer's house?" she asked as she unwrapped a wedge of Parmesan.

"Yep," I said. "How did you know?"

"Min called about a half hour ago."

I kept chopping. The thing about growing up in Belmont was that all the moms knew each other. So when you were having a fight with some kid, if one mom knew about it, all the moms did. Sometimes the moms even tried to end the fight for you, like back in fourth grade when Riley was mad at Tabitha, and Riley's mom invited Tabitha and her mom over to "talk it out." (It didn't work; not only did Tabitha and Riley stay mad at each other, but also Tabitha blamed Riley for getting her in trouble with her mom.) This kind of interfering was bad enough when you were in elementary school, but by middle school you definitely wanted the moms to back off.

"Everything okay with Archer?" Mom continued. "I've noticed he hasn't been around in a while."

"He's just really busy," I said. *Chop chop chop.* "You know, with saxophone. And video games. And homework."

"Speaking of which." Mom dumped the spaghetti into the boiling water. "I heard from your social studies teacher today. She said you're missing a bunch of homework?"

I stopped chopping. "Ms. Packer called you?"

"She emailed. I wanted to talk to you before I responded. What's going on, Hay?"

"Nothing. I'll finish them tonight."

"I mean, why are you so behind in her class? I thought you liked her."

"Oh, I do!" I decided to talk; this was different from tattling on friends. And for all I knew, Ms. Packer had already told Mom about the unit test anyway. "But the topic we're doing—it's not just boring; it's like reading about another planet!"

Mom smiled a little. "I hear you, sweet potato. But American history is part of the seventh-grade curriculum. Carter didn't love it either, and he survived."

"But Mom, I *hate* feeling like we're wasting time, just learning about this stuff because someone decided we're supposed to. Not because it *means* anything. Or has anything to do with real life!"

"Okay, so what would you rather be learning?"

"About the planet! Climate change! What's happening to the Belmont River—"

"The river?" Mom stirred the pot. "What do you mean?"

I explained about the weird results we were getting, how Mr. Hendricks was calling in an expert.

"Well, that sounds like a good idea, getting some input from a real scientist," Mom said. "But can I ask you a favor? Can you please not mention this at dinner?"

"How come?"

"What we spoke about before. Dad doesn't need you and Carter getting all worked up over upsetting topics, or the two of you squabbling at the table. Okay?"

"Sure," I said.

But I was thinking how strange it was for Mom to say this, because Carter and I weren't squabbling about the river. Actually, it was the one thing we agreed about, pretty much.

DINNER

That night at dinner, first Dad went on and on about work, and then Mom went on and on about some party invitation she didn't want to accept, even though it felt like they had no choice.

"I just don't know what to do," she told Dad. "If we don't go, they'll be offended."

"Yeah, that's the problem," Dad agreed.

"Although not an actual *problem*," I blurted.

My parents looked at me.

"Excuse me?" Mom said.

My throat burned. "I mean, it's just a little personal

issue, isn't it? Not a *problem*, because it doesn't *affect* any-thing, right? Or matter to anyone besides *you*."

"Haven, honey," Mom said, using her Patient Pre-school Teacher voice. "I'm sure you don't mean to be rude. But telling someone that what they care about isn't important—"

"Well, but it isn't, Mom! It's just a *party invitation*! Why are you making such a big deal about it, when there's so much *else* in the world—"

All of a sudden there was a rain cloud bursting inside me, and I just lost it. It was like everything I'd been think-ing about and worrying about and not-sleeping about just started swirling around in my head, and before I knew what was happening, I was coughing. And then the coughing sort of morphed into crying. Not sad crying—mad crying. A hurricane of hot, furious tears.

Mom seemed almost scared as she handed me a napkin. "Haven, honey, what's wrong? Did something happen?"

"No, and that's the problem!" I said between gulps. "Nothing is *happening*!"

Dad looked stunned. "What are you talking about?"

"Everyone is just sitting here, complaining about nor-mal boring stuff like it's the only thing that matters in the world, like everything's fine, and no one's *doing* anything!"

"About what?" Carter asked.

"You *know* what, Carter! Everything we talk about! What's happening to the oceans and the glaciers, even the river!" I wiped my face with the napkin. "I just feel so angry all the time! And frustrated. Like no one cares about anything except what's going on in their own lives! Including *you*."

"Us?" Dad said. He reached across the table to stroke my arm. "Haven, that's not fair. Or true."

"No, Dad, it is! Because if you did care, you'd do something! Or *try* to do something! Not just tell Carter and me to shut up about it!"

Mom's eyes were huge. "Haven, no one's telling you to shut up."

"You are, Mom, even if you're not saying those exact words! You keep telling me not to talk about it! Even just before, when I came home from Archer's—"

"Sweetheart, all I asked was that you didn't squabble with Carter. Or discuss upsetting things we can't solve over dinner."

"Well, how can we solve *anything* if we can't even talk about it!"

"Haven's right." Carter pushed away his plate. "Sorry if this topic upsets you guys, but that's because it's *really upsetting*."

"Yeah," I said as I blew my nose into the napkin. "But

more than just *upsetting*. Because when we're grown-ups, it'll be our planet. *Our* problem, not yours."

Carter's eyes met mine. "And what if by then it's too late to fix," he said quietly.

"Right," I said. "Exactly."

Mom's face pinched. Dad sat there frozen and blank, like he didn't know what to say.

By then my stomach was too tangled to eat, so I got up from the table and went upstairs to snuggle with Ziggy.

About a half hour later Mom and Dad knocked on my door.

"Can we come in?" Mom asked, like it was even a question.

Here we go, I thought. *Now they'll tell me to "relax," "be patient," "enjoy the process" of the world destroying itself....*

They sat on my bed. I was slumped against my pillows with Ziggy on my lap, purring and kneading his dagger-y claws into my belly.

"You shouldn't let him do that," Mom said. "He'll make a hole in your top."

"So what," I said. "I don't even like this top. It itches."

Mom sighed. "Sweetheart, Dad and I want to apologize. I think we didn't understand how strongly you felt about that subject. Carter, too. And you're right—we should all be talking about it."

"And not just talking," Dad added. "Doing something." He reached out to hug me, so I gently shoved Ziggy off my lap. "Let's all try to think how we can save energy. Turn down the thermostat, turn off the lights, take the car less—"

"Yeah, okay," I interrupted. "We *should* do all that stuff. *Everyone* should. But it's not what I'm talking about, really. And it won't solve the problem."

"Okay, sweetheart. So what do you think would?"

"I don't know! Something *bigger*." I stayed in Dad's arms longer than I had in forever, maybe since I was a little kid. It felt slightly awkward—and also comforting and safe.

Not that my parents could protect me from what was happening in the world. *To* the world. But still, at least they were listening, finally. And not telling me to change my personality.

"Sorry I blew up at you," I said after a minute. "And ruined dinner and everything."

"It's okay," Mom replied. "We're sorry we didn't get it before."

Dad held me a little longer. Then he said, "But we want you to know: anything that's important to you is important to Mom and me. Always."

"You said that to Carter too?"

"Not yet, but we will," Mom said, reaching across the bed to stroke my hair. "Also, Dad and I were thinking maybe it would be a good idea for you to talk to someone."

"Talk? You mean like to a—?"

"A therapist, sweet potato. Someone who helps kids with their worries."

I grunted. "So you mean this person will solve climate change?"

"We just mean this person will help you cope. And express your feelings."

My feelings? Ugh.

"I don't know," I said. "Maybe."

The three of us sat like that for a while. Not saying anything, just being together.

And I guess Ziggy got jealous or something, because he *mrowed* and swatted my elbow.

QUESTIONS

The next day Dr. Lopez was already at the river when we got there. I'm not sure what I'd expected when Mr. Hendricks had called her an "expert"—maybe someone with bifocals and a white lab coat. But Dr. Lopez was a young woman with very short pink hair, wearing a tomato-red hoodie, black track shorts, and waders. I couldn't tell her age, but she didn't look a whole lot older than Carter.

She was crouching on the bank, filling vials with water. As soon as our class arrived, she sprang up and showed Mr. Hendricks something on her phone.

"You sure?" Mr. Hendricks asked her.

She shrugged.

What was going on?

Riley poked my arm. "I like her hair. Don't you, Haven?"

"Yeah, definitely," I said as I watched Dr. Lopez take some photos of the river, then type something on her phone.

"All right," Mr. Hendricks called out. "Gather round, folks. Today we're lucky to have Dr. Lopez with us. Since we've been getting some unexpected results, we're asking her to observe our study and to run a few tests."

"How come?" Archer asked. "You think our results are wrong?"

"No, not at all," Mr. Hendricks said. "This is just what scientists do—confirm each other's data. We call this *replication of research*. It helps give us confidence in our conclusions."

Then that means . . . there are conclusions? I thought Mr. Hendricks said we weren't supposed to speculate!

Dr. Lopez asked to see the equipment we were using, so Ms. Alcindor brought over a few probes.

"Whoa, fancy," Dr. Lopez said as she examined the sensor we'd used to read oxygen levels. "You don't see these babies in many schools."

"They were a gift from a local business," Ms. Alcindor said. "Gemba Industries."

"Gemba? Never heard of them. Are they new?"

"Newish. They took over the old glass factory in town about a year ago."

"Really? Huh." Dr. Lopez frowned as she typed something on her phone.

I peeked at Kenji. Whatever he thought about Dr. Lopez's reaction—the "huh" and the frown, followed by typing—he wasn't showing it. But I could tell he'd been paying close attention.

Mr. Hendricks told us to get started with the physical testing, which meant I was working right near Archer. The funny thing was how chatty Archer was being all of a sudden—actually talking to me, not texting—about his level on *RoboRaptors*, the portal he'd entered, the weapon he'd unlocked, blahblahblah. It was like explaining about Em and the teasing and the pictures had lifted a weight off his chest.

Should I be relieved? I wondered as I measured the speed of the water. *Because now that he told me the truth, the weirdness is over? And poof, we're back to normal?*

Do I feel like we're back to normal?

Is "back to normal" even possible?

Think about that later, I scolded myself. *Just focus on the river!*

As Team Four began identifying macros, I could see Dr. Lopez wading in the river a few feet away, turning over rocks, taking photos, typing into her phone. To be honest, it was hard to concentrate on my work, because I kept peeking at her, wondering if she was seeing something we weren't. Drawing conclusions. Figuring out what to do.

Would she tell us what she was thinking? Even if she didn't, I had to talk to her.

Kenji was already crouched over our basin, identifying the same pollution-tolerant macros we'd seen before, so I didn't feel guilty about stepping away for a minute. I told him I'd be right back, and sloshed over to Dr. Lopez.

"Hi," I said loudly.

She blinked like she hadn't planned on talking to an actual kid. "Oh. Hello."

I spoke fast. "Can I please ask you a question? When my brother did this River Project two years ago, he found stone flies and riffle beetles—tons of pollution-sensitive macros. Also tons of frogs. And he said the water was six-point-five, just a little acidic, and the dissolved-oxygen levels were much higher. So what do you think is going on?"

Dr. Lopez nodded. "That's what I'm trying to find out."

"Okay, but what do you *think*?" For some reason, I couldn't stop myself. "Please tell me, even if you're not sure. A bad answer is better than a blank."

She raised her eyebrows. "Really? Says who?"

I almost answered *My grandpa*—but I stopped myself. I

needed this scientist to take me seriously, not decide I was a baby.

"Just something I read somewhere," I said.

"Hmm. What's your name?"

"Haven Jacobs."

"Well, Haven Jacobs, I have to tell you that what you said—a bad answer is better than a blank—is just about the *opposite* of how scientists think. We'd much rather have unanswered questions than false data or wrong conclusions."

My cheeks burned; now I felt like a total idiot. Of course that made sense! Grandpa Aaron knew plenty of stuff, but he wasn't a scientist, not even close. And really—what good would it do the Belmont River if we came up with a theory just to show we had any theory at all? If we wanted to help the river, possibly save it, we needed good answers, *right* answers, not just clipboards full of words and numbers.

As I was thinking all this, Kenji walked over in that shoulders-first way of his. I tried to ignore him, because who knew when I'd get to talk to Dr. Lopez again.

"So do you . . . have specific questions about what's going on?" I asked her. "I mean, I'm sure you do, but can you say what your questions are?"

"Well, truthfully, Haven, I'm still figuring out my questions." Dr. Lopez took a tissue out of her pocket to blow her nose. "But here's a couple off the top of my head: Was there a catastrophic event in this area—a one-time environmental accident, like a chemical spill? Or is there some ongoing cause of pollution that wasn't here two years ago?"

"Like what?" Kenji asked. He was frowning at Dr. Lopez, not even looking at me.

Dr. Lopez nodded. "I don't know. Maybe a factory that's using a toxic chemical. Even in small amounts."

Kenji ran his hand through his hair. "Although you don't *know* that."

"Right. I'm saying it's a question. And we need answers fast, before damage to the river's ecosystem becomes irreversible."

"You mean before it's too late?" I asked, almost in a whisper.

Dr. Lopez met my eyes. "Yep. That's exactly what I mean."

Now I had an icy, hollow feeling in my stomach. "Okay, but if it's true that toxic chemicals got in the river, how would that even happen?"

"Oh, different ways," Dr. Lopez answered. "It could be something like a manufacturing plant that's emptying waste into an underground tank that leaks. If that's the case, they're probably unaware it's happening. But the more obvious scenario would be if a factory was dumping its waste directly into the water."

"You mean just pouring it in?" I asked.

"Yep," Dr. Lopez answered.

"Why would they do that?"

"Why? Because it's easier than disposing of it properly. Also cheaper."

"No, that's impossible," Kenji said. "I'm *sure* it wouldn't happen."

He turned away and sloshed back over to our basins.

GEMBA

I t was like one of those scenes in a movie where only the foreground is in focus, and everything else is a blur. At lunch I barely registered that Archer had joined our table, or that Em was giggling about her Netflix series, or that Riley was watching me with worried eyes as she ate her tuna sandwich.

After a few minutes, she asked if I was okay.

"Yeah, I'm fine," I said. But then I couldn't hold it in any longer. "I think it's Gemba," I blurted.

Riley blinked. "What is? Haven, what are you—"

"The reason we're getting weird results in the River Project! I think the Gemba glass factory is doing something to the water!"

Now everyone at the table was staring at me.

"Did Dr. Lopez tell you that?" Riley asked. "When you were talking to her before?"

"Not exactly." I took a breath. "But she said that when river water gets polluted, it could be from an accident, like an oil spill or something. Which we'd have heard about in the news, right? *Or* if the pollution was happening over and over—like if a local factory was dumping toxic chemicals! On purpose!"

Em nibbled her pizza crust. "Okay, but even if that's right, it doesn't mean it's Gemba."

"But what else makes sense?" I said. "Mr. Hendricks didn't get these results last year, so that means the problem has to be pretty recent, right? And what's changed in Belmont since last year? Only Gemba taking over the factory! And practically the entire town!"

"Yeah," Riley said. "That's true, actually."

I nodded at her.

Em pressed her lips. "It still doesn't mean it's Gemba. *If* it's true that someone's polluting the river, and we don't *know* that, it could be anybody."

"Also," I said, "I know Gemba uses some really dangerous chemicals. My dad told us how they use acid to make frosted glass. What if that stuff, or something like it, got into the river?"

"Your *dad* told you?" Em said.

"He works for Gemba. He's a foreman."

"So you're accusing your own dad's company?" Em shook her head. "That's messed up, Haven."

"It's not just Haven's dad's company; it's also Kenji's." Archer scowled at Em. "That's why they moved here, so his dad could run the factory in person."

Everyone went quiet.

"Trust me, I don't want to get anyone in trouble," I said quickly. "Especially my dad, but also Kenji's, okay? And I don't want to get the factory in trouble either. I know they've done some good things, like giving us all that equipment for the River Project. But if they're also doing something *really bad—*"

"*If* they are," Em said. "That's a big *if*, Haven. And anyway, I thought you were freaking about big planet stuff. Not our town's little river."

Archer crunched on a potato chip. "Em, you think the Belmont River isn't part of the planet?"

"No, and that's not what I meant."

"So what *did* you mean? Because everything's connected, all the rivers and oceans—"

"You don't need to lecture me, Archer. For your information, I'm freaking about all this too."

I couldn't stop myself. "You *are*?"

"Well, yeah, of course I am." Em's face clouded. "I have nightmares, okay? And lately I've been wondering about having kids when I'm a grown-up. If it's fair to have them, I mean, if the planet's so messed up." She pushed away her plate. "You're not the *only* kid who thinks about this climate stuff, Haven."

"I never said I was!"

"Well, sometimes you act like it. So does Archer."

He flushed. "*What?* Em, that's totally—"

"We *all* feel scared," Riley interrupted. "I keep thinking about my grandma. What if she has another heart attack and needs to get to the hospital in a hurry? But all the roads are blocked because there's a flood or a big storm or something? So then I start thinking about scary climate stuff, and I get a bad stomachache."

Em reached across the table to pat Riley's arm before I could.

No one spoke. I realized I'd forgotten to eat my lunch, so I took a teeny bite of cheese sandwich, chewing slowly, not tasting much.

"Sorry if I sounded like you didn't care," I said to Em.

She sighed sharply. "Well, *thank* you, Haven. Because I do. I mean, *obviously*."

I flashed a look at Archer like, *Your turn.*

"Yeah, sorry," Archer muttered.

Riley turned to me. I could see she was relieved I'd apologized. "Haven, I saw Kenji coming over when you were talking to Dr. Lopez at the river. Did you say this stuff to him? About Gemba?"

"No," I told her. "But he definitely heard Dr. Lopez talk about dumping."

"How did he act?"

"He said it was impossible. Then he walked away, like he didn't want to hear it anymore."

"Well, sure," Archer said. "Because if it's true that Gemba *is* responsible, that's like a crime, right? Against the environment. I'm pretty sure you go to jail for it. Or pay a big fine, anyway."

"So we need to be extremely careful," Riley said. "And take our time to get evidence."

I felt like shouting. "But we *can't* take time, Riley! Dr. Lopez said we needed to act fast! Before damage to the river is permanent!"

"Okay, but we shouldn't accuse anyone without proof."

"All right, so what if we *got* proof?"

"How?" Riley asked.

"What if we caught them in the act? And took photos?"

"Ha," Em said. "You really think we're going to catch someone from Gemba sneaking out to the river in the middle of the day, pouring acid into the water?"

"No. I bet they do it when no one's around! Like overnight, maybe."

Em crossed her arms. "So in other words, Haven, you're saying that unless we camp out overnight, or set up spy cameras or something, *or* dig up a tank to see if it's leaking, we can't prove a thing."

"Maybe we don't need to," Riley said.

Everyone looked at her.

"Excuse me?" Em said. "Riley, you just said we shouldn't accuse them without proof!"

"So what if we *didn't* accuse them. Not directly, I mean. What if there was some way to make a statement without blaming Gemba? Or anyone else specifically. Because that's really what we care about—protecting the river, right?"

Riley's answer to everything, I thought. *Make a statement without making a statement. Talk without talking, ask without asking. No conflicts, no fighting.*

Why was everyone so afraid to do anything? Or say anything?

Just then Kenji squeezed in next to Archer. He had a small bowl of chili and a roll; no one spoke as we watched him break off chunks of roll, dip them in the chili, and eat them.

Finally he noticed the awkward silence at the table. "What were you guys talking about?" he asked.

"Nothing," Archer said.

"Nothing," Riley repeated.

She looked at me with begging eyes.

The eye message was: *Kenji is nice. And cute. Please-please-please don't make trouble for his family, Haven!*

But I was trying to help, not make trouble! Not the bad kind of trouble anyway. Why didn't Riley trust me?

I plucked my ponytail holder. Over and over, like I was playing a guitar.

Snap, snap, snap.

CLEANUP

That night, as we were cleaning the kitchen after dinner, I told Carter everything—about Dr. Lopez, my suspicions about Gemba, the fact that I had no proof and probably couldn't get any. How if we wanted to save the river, we had to act fast, because we were running out of time.

"Does Dad know you suspect Gemba?" Carter asked. He kept his voice quiet so our parents couldn't hear.

"There's no reason to tell him. Not if we're not accusing anyone, right? But it's definitely what I *think*," I added.

Carter rinsed a dish. "So do I, actually."

I almost smiled. My brother was really on my side about this—no teasing, no Lentil stuff. Maybe it was only on this one topic, and maybe it wouldn't last, but right this minute it felt really good. "I just wish we *could* prove it, though," he was saying.

"Yeah, but we can't wait for that."

"I guess." Carter shrugged. "So what's the plan?"

"I don't know! When I talked about this at lunch, Riley said maybe there's a way to accuse Gemba without accusing them."

"What does that mean?"

"I'm not sure," I admitted.

Carter poked my arm, because suddenly Mom was in the kitchen.

"You two cleaning up in here?" she asked. "Or do I have to sing the Cleanup Song?"

Carter pretended to stagger. "Not. The. Cleanup. Song. Please, Mom, anything but that!"

Mom laughed. "Well, it works great at Belmont Buddies! 'Clean up, clean up, little star. / Stop and clean up where you are.'"

"'Kay, Mom, we get it," Carter said.

But Mom wasn't done teasing. "Also: 'We will use our helping hands, helping hands, helping hands . . .'"

I grinned. "Ooh, I remember that one."

"Or we make it a game, like 'Who can clean the fast-est?' Because if you want little kids to do something, you have to make it fun."

"What about big kids?" Carter asked, raising one eye-brow.

Mom winked at me. "Big kids don't need fun, just allowance. Which they don't get if they don't do chores."

She left the kitchen. Carter and I wiped the counters and loaded the dishwasher without talking.

"Let me know if you come up with anything," he mur-mured when we were done.

I nodded. But now I was thinking about what Riley had said: *Accuse without accusing.*

And what Mom had just said: *You have to make it fun.*

"Haven, slow down," Mr. Hendricks said.

I was in his classroom the next morning before home-room. He was drinking coffee with Ms. Packer; as soon as I realized I was interrupting their conversation, I had the squirmy thought that they'd been discussing *me*, the way I was probably failing social studies.

Then I told myself that there were other things to talk about, topics more important than Haven's Lack of Home-work. And, actually, if any other teacher should hear what I had to say, it should be Ms. Packer.

So I told them everything. It came out in a tangle of words, because I hadn't slept much, and my head was buzzing.

When I finished, they both looked confused.

"You're saying you want to stage a protest?" Ms. Packer said.

"A *sort* of protest," I said. "But not really! More like a protest in disguise."

"Okay, I'm not following."

I tried again to describe my brilliant idea: we'd throw the river a party, a kind of spring festival, with food and music. "To make it fun for people," I explained. "But *also* we'll tell them about the River Project, so they understand there's a problem with the water. And if Gemba or anyone else *is* dumping chemicals, they'll see we're paying attention. Not just a bunch of middle school kids, but the whole town."

"Hmm, interesting," Ms. Packer said. "And you're asking us to be involved?"

I nodded. Then I peeked at Mr. Hendricks, who was trading a look with Ms. Packer. Not a parent look, but still a private eye conversation that didn't include kids.

"Well, we need to give this some serious thought," Mr. Hendricks was saying. "It's a cool idea, Haven, but I do have a few reservations."

"You do?" I squeaked.

"Yes. First about Gemba. I'm not saying they're blameless; we just don't know one way or the other. They have a lot of ties to the community, and they've been incredibly generous with our school. So if we're doing a big local event, we need to keep their name completely out of it."

"No problem," I said quickly. "I already thought of that! What else?"

Mr. Hendricks and Ms. Packer exchanged another look.

"We-ell," Ms. Packer said, drawing out the word so that it was almost two syllables. "*My* concern is that a festival takes planning. A whole lot of time-consuming work, Haven. And you're already significantly behind in my class. Last I counted, you're missing five assignments."

I chewed the inside of my cheek. So this *was* about my homework after all!

"But I'll make you a deal," Ms. Packer said. "I'll overlook the missing work if you'll do a report."

"A *report*?"

"On this festival. What motivated you, what you hope to accomplish, the outcome, what you learned, that sort of thing. Oral or written."

My throat burned; I fingered the ponytail holder on my wrist.

Why did I ever think Ms. Packer was un-teachery?

Here she was, turning my brilliant idea into another pointless school assignment.

Although, in a way, she *was* doing me a huge favor. Ignoring all the blanks. Not making me do Lewis and Clark.

"Okay," I said softly. "I'll do a written report. Because I really *hate* oral ones."

She nodded and looked at Mr. Hendricks.

"So one other thing," he said as he sipped his coffee.

By now I felt like punching a wall.

Why did I even bother involving grown-ups? All they do is turn your idea into a school assignment. Or make rules and conditions. No wonder the planet is dying!

"Haven, I guess you've noticed all the trash in the river," Mr. Hendricks was saying. "If people gather with food, my concern is that we'll have even more wrappers and containers that'll just end up in the water. Making the litter problem even worse."

Oh. Good point, actually! I hadn't thought of that.

"Hey, I know," Ms. Packer said excitedly. "What if we made the festival a big Clean Up the River Day? We could have all the fun stuff Haven is describing, plus a chance to share the River Project. *And* we can encourage people to wade in the water! Get their feet wet and help pick up trash!"

"Yes, definitely!" I said, grinning. "But no Cleanup Song."

My teachers stared at me. So I explained about my mom.

At last Mr. Hendricks smiled. "Deal," he said. "No Cleanup Song."

And then Ms. Packer gave me a fist bump.

FESTIVAL

Ms. Packer was right. Planning a festival for the river was more work than I'd realized—way more than I could possibly do myself.

So mostly I was happy to stand back and watch as Ms. Packer and Mr. Hendricks got a bunch of other people involved: students, teachers, parents, and even the principal, Ms. Roncione. By the end of the next week there was a food committee and an entertainment committee (someone had decided we shouldn't only have music, but also dancing, juggling, tae kwon do demonstrations, and other stuff). Plus there was a committee in charge of river cleanup. Riley and Archer started gathering rakes and gloves and shovels, and even got Xavier's parents to loan a wheelbarrow for hauling away trash.

To be honest, a part of me did feel squirmy about all these arrangements, because it seemed like people were focused mainly on food and entertainment. But I told myself that we needed these distractions, or else no one would show up. And once people were there, they'd also be learning about the River Project. And of course be cleaning litter out of the water.

While all this planning was going on, Em and Tabitha announced they were in charge of publicity. Mr. Hendricks told them he didn't want downtown Belmont flooded with paper signs ("The idea is to fight litter, not create more of it," he told them). So they made a big banner out of old sheets, which they hung in front of the library. *RIVERFEST!* it said. *FOOD! FUN! FISH!*

They'd made fancy *F*s and fancy exclamation points. I had to force myself not to point out that there were no *FISH!* in the river. Also that the rainbow glitter they'd used was actually terrible for the environment, made out of microplastics that ended up all over the place— including in oceans and rivers. (I knew this because I'd googled "glitter.")

You can't control everything, I told myself. *Isn't it good* that they made a pretty banner people will notice? Maybe it isn't perfect, but just be glad they're involved.

Even Em.

Even Xavier the Jerk.

As for explaining about the River Project, and all our weird results, Mr. Hendricks put me in charge. By "in charge" I mean he asked how I'd like to do it. I told him I'd been thinking we could have an information table displaying some of our clipboards, a few litmus strips, a macro-identification chart, a basin of macros (if any were left), and a few probes.

"And we'd be there to explain the project," I added. "What we saw this year. And what we didn't."

Mr. Hendricks gave me a thumbs-up. "I take it you're volunteering to man the table, Haven? By 'man' I mean 'run,'" he added.

"I knew what you meant. There should be a better word, though."

"*Person* the table."

"Yeah, okay." I grinned. "I'll person the table!"

"So will I," Kenji said.

I spun around. He'd been standing there the whole time, listening to this conversation.

"Sounds great," Mr. Hendricks said, giving him a thumbs-up too.

I wanted to shout *NO!* Because personing the information table, telling people how Gemba was killing the river—without mentioning Gemba!—would be hard enough. But doing it with Kenji, Son of Gemba's Boss . . .

I snapped my ponytail holder so hard it made my wrist sting.

That afternoon as I was walking home from school, Archer caught up to me.

"What's up?" I asked, making my voice sound like no big deal, the two of us had been walking home together every day.

"I just wanted to tell you that my mom's reporting on the festival," he said.

"She is? For her newspaper?"

Archer nodded.

"Oh, that's great! More publicity the better!"

"Yeah. I thought you'd be happy. Also." He looked at me. "Kenji had a big fight with his dad."

I slowed down a little. "Yeah? What about?"

"The river festival. How the idea was to explain our results. He said his dad was pretty mad about it."

I made myself breathe. "Did his dad say why? I mean, what exactly he was mad about?"

"His dad said if we got weird results, it was because we

were kids, and we didn't know what we were doing. He said Mr. Hendricks didn't know what he was doing either."

"Whoa. Okay."

"It doesn't prove Gemba's guilty, Haven."

"Well, not *scientifically*."

"Not *any* way. I'm just telling you because you're doing the information-table thing with Kenji, right? So I thought you should know Kenji stuck up for the River Project. He's not the enemy."

"Archer, I never said he was!"

"No, but I know you don't like him—"

"Who says?"

"It's obvious. You're always making faces when he talks." Archer paused. "But he likes *you*. He told me he thinks you're really smart. Anyhow."

We'd arrived at Spring Street, where Archer needed to turn left.

"Promise you won't tell Kenji I told you," Archer said.

Tell Kenji what? That I knew he had a fight with his dad about the river? That I'd heard he thought I was smart? That he . . . *liked* me? If that was even what Archer meant by "like."

I wanted to ask, but even more than that, I wanted to escape this conversation. I mean, I was grateful that Archer had told me this about Kenji, but things with Archer still felt kind of awkward. Better than they were, but definitely not back to normal.

And talking with him about another boy possibly liking me . . . ? I just couldn't.

"Sure, I promise," I said as I turned right.

EMAIL

*T*he day Ms. Packer and Mr. Hendricks agreed to my idea for a river festival, I told Carter right after school. It wasn't like I expected him to tease or call me names, because he wasn't doing that stuff to me lately. Still, I was relieved to see how excited he was. He even said he'd tell his earth-science teacher, and get all his friends to show up too.

But even after the way Mom and Dad had apologized after my meltdown, I felt too nervous to tell them about the festival. Which made no sense, really, since we weren't blaming Gemba or anyone else. So I guess I felt guilty for even *thinking* Gemba was responsible. Would Mom and Dad see the guilt on my face? My stomach knotted, and I added a rubber band to my wrist.

A couple of days after Archer told me about Kenji, I had my first appointment with April, a therapist Mom had heard about from some other teacher at Belmont Buddies. April was a youngish white woman with a nose stud and dark red hair piled on top of her head in a messy bun. She couldn't solve climate change, obviously, and she basically just listened when I told her about the RiverFest. But afterward my stomach unknotted a teeny bit, and I decided I wouldn't mind talking to her again.

Also that afternoon: the principal sent an email to all the parents at our school. Not only did Ms. Roncione invite everyone's family to the festival, but she wrote that the whole thing was my idea: *The brainchild of one of our seventh graders, environmental activist Haven Jacobs.*

Environmental activist? Eep. I could just imagine what Em would say about that description.

At dinner Mom and Dad seemed a little confused.

"I've been getting texts all afternoon from Min," Mom said. "She's asking a million questions about this river event, and I keep telling her I don't know anything. How long have you been planning this, Haven?"

"Not long," I said as I blew on my rice. "It just kind of came together."

Mom ladled some spicy lentil curry onto my plate. It was my favorite meal she cooked for the family, one of the only veggie dishes that we all ate.

"How come you didn't tell us, sweetheart?" she asked.

"I told April," I said, although right away I could hear how that sounded wrong. Like, *I told her but not you, Mom.* "Anyway, it's not that big a deal."

"Are you kidding, Haven?" Dad said. "It's a *huge* deal! For the whole town! You came up with this all on your own?"

"No, not exactly." I swallowed some curry. "I talked with my friends. And with my teachers. Ms. Packer had the idea for the river cleanup."

"Don't forget me," Carter said. "You talked to me, too."

"True, I did."

Mom and Dad shouldn't have been shocked to hear this, but I could tell that they were. It was like they still couldn't believe my brother and I had non-squabbling conversations about things.

"Well," Dad said, glancing at Mom. "I think—I'm sure we *all* think—this is just really terrific, Haven. And we're so proud of you!"

"You are?"

"Oh, you bet." Dad put down his fork. "You know, when I was a little kid, we used to catch trout in the Belmont River and eat it for supper. These days I wouldn't trust *anything* from that water. It's really sad to see how much it's changed."

Carter and I traded a look. If Dad was happy about the festival, that had to mean he didn't know about any dumping, right? Which didn't mean Gemba was innocent, only that Dad was. Still, it was a giant relief to know that!

A strange thought popped into my head right then: *Poor Kenji. It must have been awful for him to see his dad's reaction. Doubting our results. Saying we didn't know what we were doing, just because we were kids. What would Kirima Ansong have said to that?*

"I wonder if I can get my preschoolers involved somehow," Mom was saying.

"Sure!" I was so relieved about Dad I almost shouted. "Little kids care about this stuff too! Maybe they could perform a song—something riverish like 'Row, Row, Row Your Boat'! And then all their families would show up at the festival!"

"Oh, I don't think you need to worry about attendance, Haven," Carter said. "A *ton* of kids at my school already signed up."

"Signed up? What do you—"

"Yeah, my earth-science teacher posted a sign-up sheet to clean the river. It got filled in like an hour. And plenty other kids say they're coming also." Carter grinned at me. "Can you please pass the bread, O Fearless Environmental Activist?"

"Not funny, Carter," I said, grinning back at him.

By now I was starting to think this festival thing might be a big deal after all. And for the first time since I saw that scary penguin video, I felt the tiniest twinge of hope.

EM

With a week to go until the festival, it was like all the planning sped up. Ishaan's mom ordered tees that said CELEBRATE RIVERFEST! Tabitha and some of her friends gave a presentation at the elementary school to get the little kids excited about the festival. Zeb Waller's family bought canvas gloves for everyone who was doing the cleanup. Shane Callaghan's uncle said he'd set up a pizza truck on festival day; when Brenna heard this, she said her parents would get an ice cream truck too.

At lunch Em bragged how she and her mom got Dough Re Mi to donate cookies and brownies for anyone who cleaned the river. ("Our dough-nation to a good cause," they said.) She also had the idea for a rubber-duck race, so little kids could see how fast the river ran. I had to admit this seemed cute, the sort of activity Mom would probably appreciate.

"Em's really into this festival," Riley said as the two of us walked to PE.

I shrugged. "Yeah, I guess."

"Oh, but she is! She keeps talking about it, and asking what else she can do to help. I think she feels bad she's not in our science class." When I didn't respond, Riley added quietly, "You know, Haven, when you first mentioned Gemba, Em was definitely negative about the whole thing. But she isn't anymore."

"Why? Because we're doing a festival? And that sounds fun to her?" I rolled my eyes.

"No, because she thinks saving the river is important! Em's family is really into nature; they go kayaking and bird-watching and stuff."

"Huh," I said.

Riley nodded. "I know she acts like nothing bothers her. But I've been hanging out with her a lot lately, and she's pretty sensitive. Not just about climate things. About people, too. Including you."

All of a sudden something occurred to me: Em was

the one who'd told me about the rubber-band-on-the-wrist thing. How did she even know about it? She hadn't said. Could she possibly be a nail biter also? It was hard to imagine Em as nervous or "sensitive," even if she did have nightmares about climate stuff. Also: Riley had been hanging out with Em "a lot lately"? How come I didn't even know this?

Maybe because I'd been obsessed with the river festival. And thinking about Archer. And Kenji. And of course Dad.

The way Riley was watching my face, I wondered if she could read my thoughts. Not that my thoughts were ever that hard to read.

"Look, Haven," she was saying, "I agree Em's been a little obnoxious with you sometimes. I'm not saying she's perfect, or that she's my new best friend or anything. I just don't want you to think she's evil, you know?"

And Kenji is not the enemy.

Why does everyone need to tell me this?

"Sure, whatever," I said, like I was the kind of person who didn't overreact, didn't take everything to the extreme. Was totally comfortable leaving things blank, having more questions than answers.

RUBBER BAND

Exactly three weeks and one day after I met with Mr. Hendricks and Ms. Packer and told them my idea for a protest in disguise, it was festival day. All week the weather had been terrible, rainy and foggy and much chillier than it should have been for the end of May. *Climate change weather,* I told myself. Like we needed more proof that the planet was in trouble.

But on Friday afternoon the sun came out, and by Saturday morning the weather was perfect, warm and bright. The kind of temperature you expected for Memorial Day weekend. The kind of day that meant summer was officially here, whatever the calendar said.

At seven o'clock that morning, Dad drove me over to the river. The festival was supposed to start at ten—but I wanted to help Mr. Hendricks and Ms. Packer, make sure all cleanup equipment was ready to go, and get all the stuff we needed for the information table set out just right.

I'd felt guilty for asking Dad to wake up so early on a Saturday, but he seemed happy to do it.

"It's not every day your daughter's an environmental activist," he teased, kissing my cheek as we got in the car. "I'm really proud of you, Hay. Have I told you that lately?"

"Yeah, you have." I smiled at him. But my stomach was squirming. What if Dad realized the whole thing was basically about Gemba? Would he be proud of me, or furious—like Kenji's dad?

We got to the river at five after seven. No one was there.

Don't panic—it's early! You know some people are definitely coming, like Carter's earth-science class and Mom's preschoolers.

"Well, Haven, looks like you have your pick of spots," Dad said. "Where should we set up your info table?"

"I don't know. I think we should wait for Mr. Hendricks and Ms. Packer."

"Sounds good," Dad said. He glanced at his watch. "I could use some more coffee, though. What if I popped over to Dough Re Mi; I think they're open this early on a Saturday. Are you okay by yourself for a few minutes?"

"Sure." I fingered my rubber band. "Could you please get me a blueberry muffin?"

"You got it," he said, and drove off.

Where is everybody? What if I have the date wrong? Or everyone else does? Or they forget to come? Or decide not to?

I twanged the rubber band.

A few minutes passed.

A car drove up. Someone got out and waved goodbye to the driver.

It was Em, wearing shorts and flip-flops.

Twang, twang, twang.

"Hi, Haven," she called out. "Are we the only ones here?"

"So far," I said.

"Well, don't worry. My little sister's Brownie troop is coming, and so's my brother's soccer team. And I knocked on all the doors on my street to tell our neighbors!"

You did?

"That's really great," I said. I almost added *thank you*— but I didn't, because of course she wasn't doing *me* a favor.

Awkward silence.

Twang, twang.

"So I heard you go kayaking," I blurted.

Em blinked. "Yes, my whole family does. How did you know?"

"Riley told me. Also that you bird-watch?"

"Yeah, my dad's obsessed with raptors. I'm not in love with the hunting, though."

"Oh, I know! My dad and my brother like to fish." I made a *barf* face.

"Yeah, the killing part is really gross. But I still think falcons and hawks are cool." She flipped her hair over her shoulder. "Not as cool as *penguins*, though, right, Haven?"

Wait, what? I felt slapped.

Riley would want me to please-please-please not react to what Em just said. But the need to say something—finally!—was un-ignorable, like an itchy cat scratch.

"Em, what's your problem?" I said.

"Excuse me?"

"Why do you always make fun of me? Or act like every-thing I say is wrong? Just because *one time* I reacted to a penguin video—"

"Haven, all I meant—"

"I'm just *really sick* of it, you know? Riley says you can be nice, and I've seen how you are with her. So why are you nasty only to *me*?"

Em's mouth shrank. She didn't answer.

Then she did. "All right, Haven, you really want to hear?"

It's because you hate me, okay? And there's nothing I can do to change your mind."

I stared at her. "What? Where'd you get *that* from?"

"Omigod, seriously? It's so obvious! The way you only talk to Riley, and make a face if I try to be in the conversation. The way you never save me a seat in the lunchroom. Or invite me anywhere."

Was she joking? "Em, no one has to save you a seat because Riley always does! And how come *you* didn't invite *me* to your sleepover?"

"Because I knew you wouldn't come!"

"Oh." I swallowed hard. "Well, maybe I would have, if you'd asked."

As soon as I said these words, I wondered if they were true. And I think Em was wondering this also, because she didn't answer. So for a few seconds we both just stood there, avoiding eye contact.

Luckily, that was when Dad drove back.

"Hey, my dad's here," I mumbled, and ran over to our car.

"Muffin delivery, straight out of the oven, "Dad announced as he handed me a still-warm muffin wrapped in a napkin. "You okay?"

"Fine. There's this girl from my class here." I shrugged. "We aren't friends."

"Her loss," Dad said lightly. "You want me to stick

around? I think I saw a van unloading stuff for the festival." He pointed behind me.

Sure enough, Mr. Hendricks was getting out of a blue van that said BUDGET RENTALS. As soon as he saw us, he waved. "Good morning, Haven! Are you Mr. Jacobs? Can you folks give me a hand? We have some tables in the back, and folding chairs. I asked the high school football team to help with the setup, but looks like they're running late."

"No problem," Dad said. He got out of the car and gave me a quick hug. "Forget that girl," he said in my ear. "You're not here to socialize, right? Why *are* you here?"

"To save the river," I murmured.

"Exactly. So go save it, Haven Jacobs."

DOOMSCROLLING

Three hours later, so many people were crowding the riverbank that I felt silly for ever having worried about attendance. We had high schoolers, middle schoolers, elementary schoolers; parents, grandparents, babies. People in wheelchairs, in strollers, on bikes, and on skateboards. People walking dogs. You could tell that most of the crowd had turned out for the food and entertainment, a way to celebrate the start of a three-day weekend, also the unofficial start of summer. But a lot of them had come to do the river cleanup—so many that Ms. Packer had to start a wait list, and Mr. Hendricks had to call the hardware store to get more rakes and bags for waste.

So I told myself that I didn't need to feel squirmy about all the *fest* stuff in the RiverFest. We were accomplishing something important, even with all these distractions.

My worries about personing the info table with Kenji turned out to be pointless too, mainly because we were both so busy explaining our results in the River Project that we didn't have time to talk to each other. It wasn't that tons of people were crowding our table to hear about macros and probes, but the few who did were super interested, and asked a bunch of questions.

"Holy crap," Carter said when he got to the front of the info table. "This place is out of control."

I grinned. "Yeah, it is. Have you seen Mom and Dad anywhere?"

"Dad's helping with the river cleanup. Mom's with her preschoolers, doing the rubber-duck race. They sang 'Itsy-Bitsy Spider' before; it was cute. Now there's some guy juggling bowling pins, and two old ladies playing ukes."

Kenji squinted. "You're Haven's brother?"

"Yep," Carter said. "The one and only. You guys hungry? I could get some pizza from the truck."

"Thanks," Kenji and I said at the same time.

Carter nodded and took off.

"Your brother's nice," Kenji said.

"Sometimes," I admitted. "He really cares about the river. And the planet."

When Kenji didn't answer, I looked at him. "Do you have brothers or sisters?"

He shook his head. "Nope. My parents just freak out about me."

"They do? What about?"

"Everything. School. Screen time. My guitar."

I don't know why that surprised me. "You play the guitar?"

"Yeah, electric. Mostly classic stuff, like from the nineties, so you'd think my dad would be into it, right? But he says it's a waste of time."

"I'm sorry. I mean, that he says that to you."

"Yeah, well. He doesn't approve of a lot of things I care about. Like being here today."

We were getting close to dangerous territory. But I had to keep going.

"Why doesn't he want you to be here?" I asked, trying to keep my face as blank as possible. "At the festival, I mean."

"He says people exaggerate how bad things are with the planet. And that Mr. Hendricks is teaching us fake science. I keep telling my dad he's wrong, Mr. Hendricks is a great teacher, so we're always fighting."

I decided not to say I'd heard about the fighting from Archer. "What about your mom?"

"She always agrees with my dad. Even when she probably doesn't." Kenji paused a few seconds. "Anyhow, I think saving the river is really important. And that we should do whatever we can."

"So do I," I said.

Our eyes met for a second. Two seconds.

Does he suspect Gemba too? It feels like there's stuff he doesn't want to say. About his dad?

"There you are, Haven! We've been looking all over for you!" Now Min was in front of the info table with Archer, who had a streak of mud on his cheek. "Getting a lot of traffic, I hope?"

"Not really. But some," I said.

"Mostly to check out the sensors," Kenji said. "Like they're high-tech toys."

"Well, they *are* pretty cool," Archer said. "Do you tell them your dad's company donated them?"

"No. Why would I?" Kenji's eyes narrowed.

Archer and I traded a quick look.

"Okay, well, Haven," Min said loudly. "Ready for a short interview?"

"Sure! Do you want to do it here?"

Min smiled. "Oh, it won't be with me! I've known you

since you were a baby; it's not good journalism for me to interview you myself! My editor's assigned this to a new reporter,
Lauren Bicks. Don't worry, she's very nice; I've already intro-
duced her to your mom, and she says it's fine with her if you're
willing. Can I tell Lauren you're available now?"

I looked around. The only person heading over to
the info table was Carter, carrying two slices of pizza on
greasy-looking paper plates. And the whole point of this
festival was to get attention for the river, wasn't it? It would
be silly not to do an interview, if it meant more publicity.

"Sure, why not," I said.

About five minutes later, Lauren, a young dark-haired
woman with dragon tattoos covering both of her skinny,
pale arms, shook my hand and asked if we could go somewhere quiet. I hadn't assumed I'd have to leave the info
table, so for a second I hesitated. But right away Archer
said he'd be fine hanging out with Kenji—and by now I figured that anyone who wanted to hear about the River Project had already stopped by anyway. So I took one last bite
of pizza.

"Let's go," I said.

Lauren and I walked for about five minutes, chatting
about random stuff, mostly—my favorite subject at school,
what I did in my free time, if I had any pets. I told her about

Ziggy; she told me she had a chihuahua named Pimento who understood like a hundred human words.

"Including 'bagel,'" she said, laughing. "If I tell him, 'Go get me a bagel,' he jumps up on the counter and grabs one in his teeth!"

"Seriously? My cat doesn't do anything like that."

"Because he's a cat! It's against company policy to obey commands."

I laughed at that. Lauren was nice, I decided. Maybe this interview would actually be fun.

But when we got to the bench where I'd sat with Mom, her face got serious. First she asked if she could take my picture. I wasn't expecting this, so when she snapped the photo, my eyes probably looked kind of startled.

Then she asked if she could record the conversation. "It's easier than taking notes, and this way I don't misquote anybody," she said.

I told her it was fine.

She placed her phone on the seat between us. "So, Haven Jacobs," she said. "Can you tell me what gave you the idea for this festival?"

I talked about the River Project, our weird results, all the garbage in the Belmont River.

Lauren's smile was friendly, encouraging. "I guess what I'm really asking is why it matters so much to *you*."

So then I explained about the penguin video, how much it upset me, how I couldn't get it out of my mind. How I couldn't focus on social studies (and would probably fail, unless I wrote a report). How I couldn't sleep. How I had a nervous stomach. How I kept biting my nails—so badly they bled. How I couldn't stop reading about the glaciers, and the bees, and the frogs. Especially the frogs.

"Yeah, that's called doomscrolling," Lauren said. "I've been doing it a lot lately too. I'm trying to control myself better, but it's really hard, right? What about your friends?"

"My friends?" I thought. "Well, to be honest, it's been kind of weird with them lately. There's this one girl who hates me, but she thinks I hate *her*. My best friend likes her, for some reason. And at least my friend Archer is talking to me again, but I wouldn't say things are back to normal with us, exactly."

Lauren nodded. "Sorry, Haven, I wasn't clear. What I mean is, do your friends have the same feelings as you? About the climate crisis, and the planet. And the Belmont River."

Of course that was what she'd meant; now I felt like an idiot.

"Well, maybe I'm hyper-obsessed these days, but other kids are definitely worried too," I said. "Kenji says he's been fighting with his parents. My friend Archer plays games so he won't have to think about it, and my friend Riley gets stomachaches. Also this other girl named Em—she's not my friend, really—says she's having bad dreams about the planet. And maybe doesn't want babies when she's a grown-up, because who knows about the future." I looked at Lauren. "You can't put that in the article."

Lauren smiled again. "Last questions. How long have you lived in Belmont, Haven?"

"My whole life. Twelve years."

"And you think the problems with the river started fairly recently?"

"Mr. Hendricks says he got different results when his class did the River Project last year. And when my brother did the project two years ago, there was other wildlife, including frogs. So yes."

"That's so interesting. I'm wondering what's changed in Belmont over the past year. Besides the new Gemba factory, I mean."

All of a sudden my arms had goosebumps. "I can't think of anything," I said.

SIDEBAR

By the time we returned to the river, the festival was pretty much winding down. Ms. Packer was directing Xavier and some other kids to pick up trash from the food trucks, all the greasy paper plates and napkins that people had tossed on the grass, along with the disposable gloves from the river cleanup. Mr. Hendricks was taking the sensors off the info table, and the high school football team—which had finally shown up—was loading tables and chairs into the rental van.

Lauren Bicks shook my hand, thanked me for chatting

with her, and took off—before I could ask when she'd write her article.

And right away Riley came running over, squeezing me in a hug. "Archer said you were being interviewed? Omigod, Haven, that's so cool!"

"I guess." Something about the interview—I couldn't say what—had started giving me a stomachachy sort of feeling. *Maybe I shouldn't have done it,* I thought. Or I should have insisted on talking only to Min. Or made my parents be there with me. Not that they could have helped me answer those questions, though; Lauren wanted to hear *my* thoughts. *My* feelings. Which I had the right to express, didn't I?

"Well, you should feel proud!" Riley shouted. "Today was the best!"

Now Tabitha and Brenna had joined us, and I could see Em following behind.

"It was ah-ma-zing," Tabitha said. "So many people came—more than we thought, right? Everyone loved the food! And the music!"

"Yeah, and they cleaned a ton of trash out of the river," Brenna said. "The water looks beautiful now! This whole thing was really such a great idea, Haven."

Em opened her mouth like she was about to say something—maybe something nice—but just shrugged instead.

"Thanks," I said. "But it wasn't *all* my idea."

"Oh, come on," Em said. "Don't be so modest, Haven."

If this was a compliment, it actually sounded like criticism.

"What a great success!" Ms. Packer had joined us. She looked tired but happy. "Well done, all of you—especially Haven!"

I smiled and said thank you. But I was thinking: *How much did we accomplish?* People had a good time, and they waded in the river to pick up litter. But they left even more litter on the grass, and some of that would end up in the water.

Did any of these people understand about the chemicals—all the stuff they *couldn't* see?

And did Gemba get that our whole town was watching?

That it wasn't just a bunch of middle school kids who didn't know what they were doing?

That night for supper we went to Mumbai Gardens, my favorite Indian restaurant. "To celebrate," Dad said.

I ordered all my favorite dishes—samosas, curried chickpeas and cauliflower, garlic naan—smiling as Mom described her preschoolers' performance and the rubber-duck race, nodding as Dad went on and on about what a good guy Mr. Hendricks was, how hard everyone had worked hauling garbage from the river.

Even Carter kept saying what a great day it was. When we got home after the restaurant, he asked if I wanted to play *Blaster Force 7*. I said yes, both because Carter hardly ever invited me to play video games, and also because I was too wiped out to do anything else.

Afterward, though, I couldn't sleep—a combination of the excitement of the day plus a prickly feeling I couldn't name. For a while I did the alphabet game, listing foods that started with R: *radishes, rutabaga, rhubarb, rye bread, rice, ricotta, raspberries, raisins, ramen, Red Delicious apples* . . .

Then I got out of bed and turned on my phone.

No texts from Archer or anyone else.

Should I doomscroll? Maybe not.

Instead I typed: *Belmont River*.

The first thing that came up was Min's article in the Belmont Bee:

RiverFest Draws Local Crowds

Hundreds from Belmont and nearby towns gathered at the Belmont River today to take part in a festival that celebrated the river and drew attention to its litter-filled water. As locals cheered performers ranging from singing preschoolers to seniors playing ukuleles, and sampled pizza, ice cream, and assorted treats from food trucks, others waded into the river to remove trash.

The event was inspired by an annual study of the Belmont River by Belmont Middle School science teacher Adam Hendricks. Haven Jacobs, a seventh-grade student at Belmont Middle School, had the idea for the festival after becoming concerned about the condition of the river. (See sidebar.)

Omigod, that's me! I thought. *What's a sidebar?*

I scrolled frantically.

At last I found it. A box with the headline SEVENTH GRADER GRIPPED BY ECO-ANXIETY. The writer was Lauren Bicks. There was the photo of me with huge, shocked eyes. Underneath the photo it said this:

Seventh grade should be a year of soccer games and sleepovers. But for one Belmont Middle School student, it's a time of insomnia, stomachaches, and out-of-control nail biting. The cause? Nothing less than the state of our planet.

Describing her reaction to a video about the climate crisis, shown in her Belmont Middle School science class, Haven said: "It was like a lightning bolt for me. After I saw that video, I couldn't think about anything else."

She began doomscrolling in the middle of the night, watching videos about melting glaciers and disappearing fauna, including frogs and honeybees. Her schoolwork suffered; she reports "almost failing social studies." She experienced stomach problems—cramps and diarrhea. And she began biting her nails so much that they bled.

Mental health professionals refer to symptoms like Haven's as "eco-anxiety": a feeling of hopelessness and dread about impending environmental doom. How prevalent is eco-anxiety among today's kids? It's impossible to say, although Haven says that among her friends, one boy copes by zoning out on video games, a girl has stomachaches, and another boy is fighting with his parents. Outside Haven's own social circle, a girl Haven identifies only by initial says she has recurring nightmares about climate change.

Explaining what inspired her to come up with the idea for the river festival, Haven said: "Kids have this feeling that grown-ups aren't doing enough to save the planet, and that makes us feel desperate, like there's nothing we can do to make a difference. I'm just hoping the festival helps focus people on the river, so we can protect it before it's too late."

How would protecting the Belmont River impact the rest of the planet? "I'm not sure," Haven admitted. "But I know everything in nature is connected. And I'm really worried about our town."

According to Haven, the "weird results" seen by her science class when they tested the river water this spring are fairly recent. Did she have any theories about the source for those "weird results"— besides the introduction of the new Gemba glass factory in town?

Haven's expressive face looked troubled as she thought about her answer.

"I can't think of anything else," she replied.

CHEESE SANDWICH

*O*h no. Oh no.

  This can't be happening.

I can't be reading this.

Omigod. Omigod.

What should I do?

What time is it?

5:35.

I texted Archer:

Are you awake?? I need to talk!!!

I waited five minutes, but he didn't answer. And of course I couldn't just sit there forever, like a stuffed

Pikachu—so I threw on a tee and yoga pants and grabbed my backpack. In the kitchen I made myself a cheese sandwich and poured water into one of Dad's commuter cups. Then I crammed the sandwich and the cup into my backpack.

And started running.

ECO-ANXIETY

*E*ven though it was the Sunday of Memorial Day weekend and the sun was already up, the air that morning was so chilly I wished I'd brought a hoodie. *But so what,* I told myself. *I deserve to be cold! Like I'm in Antarctica before it melted away!*

I made myself eat the cheese sandwich, mostly to have something to do.

I drank some water. Not too much, though, because there wasn't anywhere to pee.

At last my phone beeped. A text from Archer. Finally!

What's going on, Haven? Are you okay?

No, I'm not, I typed with frozen fingers. I'm at the river—the station where we did the River Project. Just get here as fast as you can!!!

Tell me what's going on, he texted.

No! Too much to say & my fingers are cold.

You want to call?

NO. Just hurry!!

Then I thought of something. Don't tell your mom! Don't ask her to drive you—just get here fast!

Pause.

Haven, you sure you're okay??

YES. NO. Just come, Archer, PLEASE

Be right there, he replied.

I twanged my rubber band.

Seventeen minutes later Archer was at the river, in sweatpants and a faded Zelda tee. His cheeks were pink; his hair was damp with sweat. By the way he was panting, I could tell how hard he'd worked to get here fast.

"What's wrong?" he asked immediately.

I showed him the sidebar on my phone. He read it, frowning, then looked up at me.

"Okay," he said. "So what are you thinking?"

"I'm thinking this reporter—who your mom said was really nice—totally betrayed me! Archer, I *swear* I never blamed Gemba. This reporter did!"

Archer stared at my phone. "Well, yeah. I mean, that's pretty much what it says in the article, right?"

"But she makes it sound like I agreed!"

"Is this *exactly* what you said—'I can't think of anything else'?"

I nodded. "But I didn't mean that I was accusing Gemba! Archer, I promised Mr. Hendricks and Ms. Packer I wouldn't." I couldn't help it; I burst into tears. "And now my dad will read this, and he's so proud of me! You should have seen him yesterday—he was so happy and excited about the festival! What if this interview gets him fired?"

"I'm sure it won't."

"You are? Well, *I'm* not! Kenji's dad sounds kind of scary. And Kenji—he's already fighting with his dad about the festival. This will just make everything worse! For Kenji, I mean."

Archer handed me a dirty, crumpled tissue from his sweatpants pocket. "So then . . . you *don't* hate him?"

"Of course I don't." I blew my nose. "*And* that reporter made it sound like I'm this basket case. 'Gripped by eco-anxiety.'"

"Haven, that's nothing to be ashamed of."

"My 'expressive face.' What's *that* supposed to mean?"

"Well, you do make a lot of faces."

I groaned. "Do I really need the whole town to know about my stomach? And that my nails are bleeding?"

"I don't know," Archer said slowly. "Don't you think it could be a good thing?"

"A *good* thing? How?"

"I mean, it's hard to get grown-ups to care about the planet. But they do care about *us*, right? So if they know we're freaking out, walking around with chewed-up fingers—"

"I'm not chewing my *fingers*, Archer. Just my nails. And I'm not even doing it so much anymore."

"You get what I'm saying. Grown-ups should know how kids feel. Eco-anxiety, or whatever you call it. I think it could help."

"Yeah, maybe." I was still feeling too desperate to agree that he might have a good point. *"Plus* that reporter wrote that Em's having nightmares. And that I don't consider her my friend."

Archer frowned at my phone. "She wrote that? Where?"

"She said Em was 'outside my social circle.' When I said Em, the reporter must have thought I was saying the letter *M*! I told her not to mention other kids, but she did anyway. At least she left out about Em not wanting babies." Now I couldn't help it; I started chewing my thumbnail. "Everyone's going to be so mad at me for talking about them! To a reporter! Why did your mom make me get interviewed?"

"Haven, come on," Archer said. "My mom didn't *make* you. I was right there when she asked you about it, so I heard the entire conversation. And I really don't think this article is that bad. I mean, it explains how kids feel, and why we did the festival, doesn't it?"

I sat on my hands so I couldn't bite my nails. "That's another thing."

"What is?"

"The festival. Everyone keeps saying what a big success it was. But it wasn't."

"What do you mean?"

"Archer, the whole thing was basically entertainment. Socializing on a beautiful spring day. It didn't *accomplish* anything."

"Well, we did get a bunch of litter out of the river."

"And then made more trash all over the grass. We should have used the kind of plates and cups you can compost! Besides, litter isn't the actual problem with the water, is it." I sighed. "I just feel like we blew it, you know? We had a chance to make a statement about pollution, about chemicals killing the wildlife, and we were too scared. *I* was too scared. So instead we threw a party."

Archer didn't argue. We sat there for a few minutes, watching two squirrels squabble at each other in a tree.

Finally he looked at me. "Okay, so what do you want me to do? I mean, about the article."

"Can't you talk to your mom? Tell her to make the newspaper take it down?"

Archer went quiet. Then he chose his syllables. "Haven, it's not up to her; she's not the editor. And even if it's taken down online, the newspaper's already printed. We got our copy; I saw it in the driveway when I ran out just now."

I hugged my knees. If Archer's newspaper had been delivered, that meant our family's had too. This article was in driveways and mailboxes *all over town*. In other nearby towns also.

"I could still call Mom, though," Archer said. "Ask her to pick us up and take you home."

"I'm not going home."

"You're not?"

"I'm staying right here."

"What do you mean?"

"I'm doing a protest—a *real* one this time! To protect the river! And I refuse to leave."

Archer groaned.

"What?" I asked. "Why are you making a noise?"

"Because you can't protest all by yourself, Haven! If you're not leaving, then neither am I."

"You're not?"

He shook his head. I looked at him, this kid I'd known longer than almost anyone outside my family. Everything about Archer felt safe, familiar. Even the scent of his shampoo.

"Archer, you're a good friend," I said softly. "For a while you weren't, though. You hurt me *a lot*. And when I came over to your house, you didn't apologize; you just said I was too sensitive."

"I know." His shoulders slumped. "I wish I'd stood up to Xavier and those other kids better. And not telling you about the pictures—I really messed up, didn't I."

"Yeah, you did. Also, being sensitive isn't a *bad* thing. If some macros weren't sensitive, we wouldn't know about the river!"

Archer didn't answer.

"You think I'm wrong?" I demanded.

"Well, what you just said isn't exactly accurate, you know? We did have other data too, besides the wildlife observation. The oxygen levels, the litmus testing—"

"Come on, Archer, you get what I'm saying!"

"All right, yes, I do. I'm sorry I said that, Haven. About you being too sensitive, I mean."

I finally felt like smiling. And breathing.

"Eh, it's okay," I told him. "I guess we all get do-overs."

SHEETS

*A*rcher and I sat on the grass playing *RoboRaptors* on his phone. And he was right—it was a terrible game, so terrible it was actually funny. Every time you scored a point, a voice would holler, "Robo-tastic!" And the bird sounds were obviously just some guy going "Squawk, squawk!"

But I was glad for the distraction, and after about a half hour of *RoboRaptors*, I felt calmer. But just as determined as when I first got there.

Every fifteen minutes we could hear church bells from behind the baseball field. When they rang at seven thirty, Archer said, "You know, if we're really doing this, it would be better to have more people, don't you think? And signs, so everyone knows *why* we're here. And we should tell our parents, right? Ask them to bring food and stuff."

Of course he was right; I really hadn't been thinking straight. I mean, I'd just run out of the house this morning, without even leaving a note.

I called my mom's phone. She answered with a muffled voice, like I'd woken her. Which I probably had; I'd been awake for so long that I'd forgotten it was a holiday weekend.

"Haven, you're *where*?" she shouted.

I told her I was with Archer, and we were both fine. That we were at the river, protesting chemicals in the water, and could she please bring me a hoodie? Also granola bars and a banana. Maybe some crackers and a jar of peanut butter too. And a blanket to sit on. Oh, and if we had any extra sheets—

"*Sheets?*" she repeated. "What are you *talking* about?"

I heard my dad's voice then. "Heather, what's going on? Where's Haven? Is she all right?"

"She's at the river with Archer. They want sheets."

"What? Why?"

Okay, so now Dad was wide awake too, obviously.

"Mom, we just want to make signs," I said quickly. I was thinking about the banner Em and Tabitha had made for the RiverFest. We didn't need anything glittery—we didn't *want* anything glittery—but it did need to get attention.

"Well, you can't have our bedsheets, sorry." Mom paused. "But there's some extra poster board you could have. Belmont Buddies used it for our Mother's Day celebration—"

"Poster board is perfect," I said quickly. "What about spray paint?"

"Preschools never use spray paint," Mom said. "Only crayons and markers."

"Okay, so please bring the markers! How soon can you get here?"

"Haven, you just woke us up! We haven't showered or had coffee—"

"Sorry," I said quickly. "Okay, no rush. We're not going anywhere anyway."

I was just about to hang up. Then I thought of something. "Oh, and don't read the newspaper, okay?"

While I was on the phone with Mom, Archer called Min. He also texted Kenji, who said his family didn't get the newspaper. (Phew, *that* was a relief!) I texted Riley, who said she'd text Em, plus her whole soccer team.

Would any of them join us? I figured Riley would, but I doubted Em. But then I reminded myself that I'd thought things were hopeless with Archer, and here he was, right beside me. Sometimes I could be really wrong about people.

At eight fifteen Mom and Dad drove up. They'd brought my favorite purple hoodie and all the food I'd asked for, plus a box of graham crackers, some string cheese, and green grapes. Also the blankets we used for picnics, eight white pieces of poster board, and two plastic bins of markers. Also sunscreen, because, you know, parents.

"You're going to stay here all day?" Mom asked, squinting in the morning sun.

"Yep, and all night, too," I said as I zipped up my hoodie. "And tomorrow and the next day, and the day after that! As long as we need to be here!"

"No way. Absolutely not, Haven!"

"Mom, we have to! If we're making a statement, we have to be serious!"

"No one's saying you aren't serious. But you can't just sleep out here forever, on the grass!"

"You can stay here tonight," Dad said, as if he were translating for Mom. "And of course we'll join you."

"You *will*?"

"Of course we will!" Mom said. "We're not letting you sleep outdoors on your own!"

"But I'm not on my own—I'm with Archer!"

"Well, I hate to break it to you, but no way two middle school kids are going to spend *the entire night—*"

"Haven, come on, okay?" Dad cut in. "We know this is really important to you."

"Then why can I stay here only one night?" I argued. "One night won't mean *anything*!"

"Haven," Dad said, looking straight into my face.

It felt like fireworks were going off in my head. I crossed my arms, squeezing my chest so I wouldn't explode.

"*What?*" I croaked. "You're going to tell me to relax? Be patient? Accept what I can't control?"

"Sweetheart, please. We're trying to be supportive."

"So then why are you making me leave? After *just one night*?"

"Because tomorrow's a holiday, but you have school on Tuesday, don't you?" Dad smiled a little. "Besides, Ziggy will miss you."

By then I knew I was losing the argument, but I couldn't stop. "Kirima Ansong's parents let her boycott school for two entire weeks! And sail from Montreal to New York to protest carbon emissions on airplanes. *And* stop traffic in front of the United Nations."

"Well, we're not Kirima Ansong's parents," Mom said. "And Kirima Ansong is seventeen. You're twelve."

"So what! We're both trying to save the planet! What difference does it—"

"*Look,*" Mom said in an end-of-argument way. "We

know how much you care about this, Haven, and we really do want to help. But there are limits."

"You can have today and tomorrow," Dad said. "And I think that's being more than fair." I definitely didn't want to cry, but now my eyes were burning, and I felt like shouting: *I thought you guys were on my side! Isn't that what you told me after my meltdown? And now you're acting like you care more about school, and what day it is on the calendar!*

This was when Archer poked my elbow and gave me a look that probably meant, *You're not going to win this fight, Haven. Just agree with them, okay?*

I balled up my hands in my hoodie pockets. "Okay, fine."

"Good," Dad said. "We'll bring over sleeping bags and tents later on. Archer, you need anything?"

"I don't know," Archer said. "I haven't really thought about it."

Mom sighed. "Does Min even know about this protest?"

"We haven't discussed any details," Archer admitted. "But she knows I'm here now. And why. And that I'm with Haven."

"Well, she's not going to be thrilled about the overnight part."

"*Mom,*" I said.

"All right, I'll try to talk to her." She sighed. "So what's the plan here, exactly?"

Archer and I locked eyes. He shrugged.

Should I say?

How could I not?

"Someone's dumping chemicals in the river," I said quickly. "We won't blame anybody; we just want to send a message to whoever's doing it that we're watching."

"That's why we can't leave," Archer said. "In case they dump during the night."

Dad looked at Mom. Then at me. "You're thinking it's Gemba," he said quietly.

EVIDENCE

I stared at Dad. "How did you know?"

"Sweetheart, it was in the newspaper," he said. "That interview you did."

"But I thought—I mean, I asked you guys not to read it!"

Mom rested her hand on my shoulder. "Haven, you really think if a kid tells her parents *not* to read the newspaper, they won't? Of course we read it!"

Now my face was on fire. "But I never told that reporter it was Gemba, I swear! *She* said it, not me!"

"Oh, that was obvious," Dad said. "And I have to say she was wrong to include it in the interview. You shouldn't write things like that without proof, or without giving Gemba a chance to respond. Frankly, I'm shocked her editor allowed it to print."

I could barely look at him. Barely talk. "But you're still going to let me protest? And stay here? Even though you could get fired?"

Dad traded a long look with Mom, then turned to me. "Haven, I should tell you that I've never seen, or heard, any evidence that Gemba is dumping toxic chemicals in the water. If I found out they were, I'd speak up about it. Loud and clear." He paused a second. "But if someone *is* dumping, they need to stop right away. Where are those markers?"

I handed him a plastic bin. Whatever Dad was thinking, whatever he'd decided right then, was the total opposite of what I'd expected. I had the strange thought that however well I'd thought I knew my parents, I'd been wrong.

"Thank you," I said in a small voice. "I was sure you'd be mad at me."

"Nah, we're cool," Dad said. He winked at Archer. "Not as cool as Kirima Ansong's parents, but . . ."

"Stop," I said, grinning. Then something occurred to me. "What about Carter? Does he know we're here?"

"He's still sleeping, but I texted him on the way over," Mom said. "I said he should get here as soon as possible. And tell his friends, too."

"Nice," Archer said.

The way his eyes had lit up, I could see he was excited that Carter would be joining us. A month ago, I probably would have been annoyed by this, like *What's so great about my brother?* But the truth was I'd changed my mind about Carter lately. I mean, mostly.

The four of us began making the posters:

DON'T DUMP ON OUR RIVER

TOXIC CHEMICALS NOT WELCOME

CLEAN WATER IS A RIGHT

NO POISON H2O

IF YOU WERE A FISH, YOU'D BE

HOME BY NOW

(The last one was Mom's contribution. It was hard for me not to point out that the Belmont River was fish-free, but I made myself keep quiet.)

Just after nine, Riley arrived with her mom, who brought a big thermos of coffee for the grown-ups, and two boxes of fresh-out-of-the-oven cinnamon doughnuts for everyone else.

"So I read the interview," Riley told me in private as the two of us split a warm, greasy doughnut. "It's not *that* bad, Haven."

"Really?" I nibbled my doughnut half. "Because *I* thought she made me sound like Ms. Eco-Anxiety."

"Well, maybe a little," Riley admitted.

I groaned.

"But that's kind of the point," Riley said quickly. "How kids are feeling about planet stuff. Grown-ups should *know* that, don't you think?"

"Yeah, that's what Archer says."

"Well, he's right. So if other kids read it—"

"They'll think, 'Well, at least I'm not as messed up as Haven.'"

Riley hugged me. Then she laughed. "You're not messed up," she said. "Although . . ."

"Although what?"

"Well, I did just get cinnamon sugar all over your back."

ALLIES

t 9:25, Em arrived with her dad, who chatted with Mom and Dad like they were all old friends. A few minutes later, three of Riley's soccer teammates showed up. One of these teammates, a girl I knew from school named Diya, came with her older sister, Tosha, who'd brought some friends from the high school—Sami and Meritt, and a boy named Jake who was on the football team. Sami and Meritt said they'd texted like a million other people, who'd probably stop by later in the morning, and too bad there weren't any more doughnuts. So right away Dad offered to drive over to Dough Re Mi to see what was left, and while he was over there, did anyone want anything else?

"More coffee," Mom told him. "Iced, please!"

"Gotcha," Dad said.

I watched them trade one of their grown-up looks that was practically a whole conversation.

At ten o'clock, I counted twenty-three people at the river, including Tabitha and Brenna. Carter showed up at ten thirty with his friend Gavin and four other basketball players, plus Ashlyn Russo, a tall, skinny white girl with neon-green bangs and too much mascara.

"Haven, this is awesome," Carter said. The way his eyes were shining at me, I could tell he meant it.

"Well, it's not awesome *yet*," I said. "We haven't *done* anything."

"Haven never takes credit," Em announced. "She's way too modest."

More praise that was actually criticism! And why was she explaining me to my own brother?

Carter narrowed his eyes at me like, *Who is this person?*

Right then I felt a gush of love toward my brother. And not just for caring about the river, or showing up with his friends.

An hour later there were thirty-seven people—painting banners, chatting, eating doughnuts (plain and jelly,

because Dough Re Mi had run out of cinnamon). Seeing everybody there, I realized I was feeling better, not as
panicky about that sidebar interview, but also desperate
to pee. So desperate I could barely think about anything
else. What did protesters do when there were no bathrooms
around? This problem had to have come up before, I told
myself.

Finally I pulled Mom aside to ask what I should do.

"Wait here—I have an idea," she said.

I watched her run across the road and enter Jonny's
Pizza. The owner's kids went to Belmont Buddies, so whenever we ordered a pizza, he threw in a free salad or some
cannoli. This time, though, Mom walked out a minute later
without any food at all.

"Okay," she told me. "I just spoke to Jonny, and he says
we can all use the bathroom as long as we're here. I told
him we'd be ordering a lot of food later, and I gave him a
nice tip, so he's more than happy to help. Go ahead, Hay,
but be careful crossing."

Em was standing a few feet away, so of course she over-
heard. "Ooh, can I come with you, Haven?" she begged.

Obviously, I couldn't say no.

Em and I crossed the road and entered Jonny's. First I
went to the bathroom; then it was Em's turn. The whole time
she was in there, I considered escaping. Because it wasn't like

she needed me to wait for her, right? Although running off, leaving her here by herself, also seemed rude. I told myself that even if Em was rude to me, I shouldn't be rude back. Especially after what I'd said about her in that interview.

That interview. Why did I do it? Why did I tell that reporter about other kids?

I'm such an idiot.

Finally Em opened the door.

"I'm really sorry," I blurted.

She raised her eyebrows. "About what?"

"Telling that reporter about you! I told her not to mention you; I didn't think she'd write about your bad dreams. And that you're 'outside my social circle' . . ."

"Haven, it's fine."

"It *is*?"

"Can I please say something? I've been thinking about this since we talked before the festival. I know the two of us don't get along so well, and I'm not saying it's totally your fault. Or totally *my* fault, either. Sometimes that's just how it is with people, right?"

I twanged the rubber band. "Yeah. I guess."

"But when something is really important, like what's going on with the river, maybe we can forget that stuff a little. The you-and-me stuff, I mean. And just . . . be on the same side about this. Kind of like teammates."

I swallowed. "Or allies."

"Right, allies."

Em looks serious, I thought. *She's not making fun of me; she actually means this.*

"Yeah, okay," I said.

For a second I worried she'd want to hug or something, but she didn't. Instead we gave each other a quick, awkward smile and headed across the road.

CHANT

When we got back to the river, Diya's mom was there, talking loudly over the yapping pug that was wriggling in her arms. "So in other words, it's okay," she was telling Diya, Riley, and Archer.

"What is?" Em asked.

Diya's mom turned to Em and me. "You kids being here, protesting. I checked with the town hall to see if you needed a permit, and they said you didn't."

A permit? Eek. I didn't even think of that!

"Yeah," she continued. "Although I have to be honest:

I'm not crazy about you being here. Any of you, including Diya and Tosha."

Diya's face crumpled. "How come?"

"Well, first of all, it's Memorial Day weekend, when we should be thinking about our soldiers instead. The timing is terrible! And also, this is how you voice your opinions? By going straight to protesting? There's so much else you could be doing instead: writing letters to the editor, circulating petitions—"

"I'm sorry, but there isn't time for that," I said with a choky voice. "The Belmont River is dying!"

Diya's mom squinted at me. "Okay, honey, but don't you think that's overreacting? The river looks fine to me! I agree, it's a little dirty, but—"

My throat felt scorched; now I couldn't even answer.

That was when I noticed Kenji, who must have arrived while Em and I were over at Jonny's. He was standing off to the side, not far from Carter and his friends, who'd obviously been watching the whole conversation.

Our eyes met for a second.

He gave me a little nod. Like: *Just let her talk, Haven. It doesn't matter.*

"Listen," Diya's mom was saying. "I'm sure you kids have good intentions, but I really don't see what you're trying to accomplish. Buster, *behave*," she snapped at her dog.

"*And* this is a small town. We're all just neighbors, right? I'm sure if we sit down and talk it over—"

Just then Mom appeared. "We think Haven and her friends are doing *great*," she interrupted loudly. "And we support them completely." Then she made a kissy face at Buster and started cooing. "Ooh, you're so adorable! Would you like a doughnut, good boy? Let's go see if any are left!"

We watched her lead Diya's mom and Buster over to the refreshments.

Carter raised his eyebrows at me. "Go Mom," he murmured, and I had to agree.

"Hey, Carter!" Now Ashlyn Russo was giving my brother a little slap on his arm. "Remember when we did the River Project in seventh grade and you put a frog in my backpack? I was sooo maaad at you." She laughed in a flirty way.

Oh right, I thought. *This is the girl Carter told me about.* Although I hadn't pictured her with green bangs.

Maybe I should have shut up then, but I couldn't. "And now they're all gone," I said.

Ashlyn stopped laughing. She blinked her smudgy eyelashes at me. "I'm sorry, what?"

"The frogs. You don't see any, right? They've all disappeared, just like the honeybees."

"Omigod, you're right." Ashlyn's face crumpled. "I *don't* see any frogs! Not a *single one*! This is *tragic*, y'all. We have to do something!"

Right away Tosha, Sami, Meritt, and Diya started a chant. Ashlyn joined it too; she was definitely the loudest.

"Where. Are. The Frogs!"

I wanted to tell them to quiet down, or maybe Diya's mom would be back to scold us. Besides, no one knew exactly *why* the frogs had disappeared—it could have been chemicals in our river, or climate change across the planet, or some other reason we didn't even know. And we were here to save pollution-sensitive macros—not just frogs!

Even though I couldn't stop worrying about where they'd all gone.

Before I could say any of this, Em, Tabitha, and Brenna were chanting also, clapping their hands and stomping on the ground.

Where. Are. The Frogs!

Where.

Are.

The—

"Hey, Haven." Archer was shouting in my ear. "Can I please talk to you a second? In private?"

"Sure," I said, relieved to escape the chanting.

The two of us walked about twenty steps, stopping near our station for the River Project.

"What's up?" I asked.

"So," Archer said. "I've been thinking. How would you feel about another interview?"

FRISBEE

"*Another* interview?" I stared at Archer. "Are you serious?"

"This time it'd be different," he said quickly. "Not with the same reporter! With my mom."

"With Min? But she said she couldn't interview me! Because she knew me!"

"I know, but I've been thinking. I bet if I explained—"

"Archer, *why* would I do an interview after that other one?"

"To spread the word! You said yourself how the festival didn't communicate anything about the river, right? So maybe if my mom wrote an article about this protest, it would get the message out better."

I twanged really hard.

"I don't know," I said.

It wasn't that I didn't trust Min; I did. But an interview meant losing control of my words again. Even if Min typed exactly what I said, even if I didn't say the word "Gemba," who knew how it would come out in print?

Although how much control did I really have anyway? The chants were getting louder every second.

This is not how it's supposed to go, I told myself.

But how *was* it supposed to go? To be honest, I had no idea.

Where. Are. The Frogs!

Where. Are. The Frogs!

Where. Are—

Over Archer's shoulder I could see Mom shouting, "Who wants pizza?" The chanting paused as kids answered: *Me! I do! Extra cheese! Sausage, please! Ooh, can we get pepperoni? What about Pepsi? Are we doing slices or pies?*

"Haven?" Now Carter had walked over to join us. "Can I ask you something?"

"Sure," I said.

"Don't take this the wrong way, okay? But . . . is there a plan?"

"What do you mean?"

"I mean, what exactly are we doing here? Besides chanting and eating pizza."

Now my stomach twisted. "We're not 'doing' anything, Carter. We're just protesting."

"Yeah, I get that." Carter shaded his eyes. "I heard that whole conversation with Diya's mom. And I'm really *not* trying to give you a hard time, Haven."

I could tell my brother meant it; he wasn't teasing, and he wouldn't call me Lentil. But in a strange way this felt even worse.

"Okay," I said. "So what *are* you saying, then?"

Carter wiped some sweat off his forehead. "I just think this whole thing is sort of . . . well, pointless, isn't it? I mean, we probably won't witness any dumping, because I doubt it happens right out in the open. And if all we're doing is chanting at each other, who even hears it besides us?"

I wanted to argue. But the words in my head weren't an argument: *If a tree falls in a forest and there's no one around to hear, does it make a sound?*

"And don't you think we should be demanding something?" Carter continued.

"Demanding?" I stared at my brother. "Like what?"

"I don't know, an investigation? So we know exactly who's responsible for the pollution? Or maybe a new law, so it doesn't happen again? Just anything specific." He glanced over his shoulder. "Anyway, I think maybe you should say something."

"To who?"

"Everyone here. So they know *why* they're here."

"You mean give a speech?" I was horrified. "Forget it, Carter!"

He shrugged. "Well, people are starting to leave. I saw Diya and Tosha leave with their mom. And that awful little dog."

I didn't answer. The way Diya's mom had been talking, it wasn't surprising, actually.

"Also those soccer girls," Carter added.

"They left? But they just got here!"

"Not really," Archer said. "They've been here for like two hours. Almost three."

Three hours? Was that possible? Not sleeping last night, getting here so early this morning, I'd pretty much lost my sense of time.

Right then the football player named Jake started tossing a Frisbee. It was yellow, one of those light-up ones that buzzed in the air, like a little kid's drawing of a flying saucer. Carter's friend Gavin made a sound like *whoop* as he caught it and flicked it back to Jake, who tossed it again as a few kids cheered.

"Haven!" Riley was jogging over. "Your parents just left with my mom to get the pizza. They said they're getting you a slice of mushroom." As she got nearer, her smile faded. "Wait, what's going on?"

"Nothing," Archer told her. "And that's like the problem. This whole thing is out of control."

Riley searched my face. "So what do you want to do?"

"I don't know!" I wailed. "Why is everything up to me?"

"Because you're in charge," Carter said quietly. "This is your protest, isn't it?"

"But it's not! It's supposed to be *everyone's* protest! The whole town's!"

I didn't know what else to say, so I took off the hoodie— why was I still wearing it in this heat?—and tied the sleeves around my waist.

Carter is right. What's the point of chanting to ourselves? Making signs no one reads?

What's the point of protesting, if no one even knows about it?

If a tree falls . . .

Just then, as the yellow Frisbee flew over our heads into the almost-summer sun, a strange thing happened. It was like I could hear Grandpa Aaron speaking to me, stroking my cheek the way he used to: *Use all the words you can think of. A blank answer earns nothing at all.*

Not the best advice for a scientist, Dr. Lopez had said.

But for me, at that moment, it was exactly what I needed.

I turned to Archer. "All right, I'll talk to Min," I said.

THUMBNAILS

While the grown-ups left to go hang out in town, we ate pizza and played games on our phones for a while. Some of the high schoolers started a game of touch football. Ashlyn played music on her iPad and a few kids, including Em and Tabitha, danced.

Not very protesty behavior. But I told myself that until Min got here, all we needed to do was pass the time.

I started planning what to say to her. I'd leave out Gemba, of course. Nothing about my friends, and nothing too personal about me. And I'd thank everyone who'd picked up litter yesterday. Then I'd give a more in-depth explanation of the River Project, so that people understood that the actual problem wasn't litter. After that I'd ask for an investigation, like Carter said. Maybe Min could interview Carter too. Ooh, and what if we took a photo, all of us holding up the posters?

Around three I asked Archer what time his mom was arriving.

"I dunno, suppertime," Archer said, not taking his eyes off his phone. "She said she's cooking us a big feast."

"Seriously?" Min was amazing, I thought—a great cook, a great journalist. Although it seemed a little funny to bring a feast to an interview, but whatever.

Around three thirty, the football game ended. I tried not to freak out as people began taking off: first Gavin and Carter's other basketball friends, then Jack and the rest of Riley's soccer friends, then Tabitha and Brenna, and finally the high school girls, all except Ashlyn.

Of course Riley could read my face. "Don't worry, I'm not going anywhere," she said. "I told you I'd stay, remember?"

"I'm staying too," Archer reminded me.

"So am I," Kenji said quietly.

I looked at him. "Your dad's okay with that?"

"Yeah, well." Kenji cleared his throat. "He doesn't know where I am, so."

"He *doesn't*? And you're just going to sleep here? Overnight?"

"Kenji, you can't," Riley said. "They'll call the police, or something."

"And then we'll all get in trouble. Maybe Haven's parents, too," Archer said.

Kenji hugged his knees. "No one's getting in trouble." he said. "And if I am, I don't care. I'm always in trouble with my dad anyway."

I traded a look with Riley, who shrugged.

And it was like something hit me in the chest: I didn't want Kenji to leave—not only because if he did, we'd be down to nine people. But also because . . . *I didn't want him to leave.*

Whatever that meant.

Although not leaving sounded dangerous. For Kenji and maybe the rest of us. Including my dad, possibly.

As I was thinking all this, Em was a few feet away from us, pacing as she talked on the phone to her mom. I couldn't hear every word, but I got the gist of the conversation: her mom wanted her to come home, and Em wanted to stay overnight.

As Em's voice got louder, it got higher and shakier. "You don't understand—this is incredibly important to me!" she was almost shouting. And: "Mom, it's so unfair! You never let me do *anything*!" And: "Everyone else is staying!"

And then: "Of course there are parents! You want to talk to them? Riley's mom, and my friend Haven's—"

I froze. *My friend Haven.* Not *my archnemesis Haven.* Not even *my ally Haven. My friend.*

So yeah, that was surprising.

The other surprising thing was that as she was talking and pacing, I could see that Em was chewing her thumbnails: first one, then the other, then the first one again. Only her thumbnails, but she was really going at them, almost like Ziggy when he was cleaning his claws. And that was when I knew that the rubber band trick was hers—maybe even something she'd invented, like my alphabet game.

I got up to stretch my legs, take a bathroom break at Jonny's Pizza, telling myself I was giving Em a little privacy. But the truth was, I didn't know how much more about Em I wanted to find out.

Not long after I got back from Jonny's, Mom and Dad returned from town to say they were going home for a bit to wash up, recharge their phones, and feed Ziggy. Also to get our tents and sleeping bags—and did I need anything?

"Just my toothbrush," I told them.

"Sure thing." Dad smiled. "I know Riley's mom is bringing a tent and sleeping bags. What about you guys? All set for the night?"

"My mom's bringing my sleeping bag when she comes over with the food," Archer said.

"Yep, she told us. I meant the rest of you."

Em made a face. "My parents won't let me stay. They're picking me up at eight."

"So unfair," Riley said, pouting.

"Yeah, I tried to convince them, but . . ." Em's voice wobbled.

Whoa, she really does care about this after all. Maybe I was wrong about Em. I mean, mostly.

"I'm okay," Kenji blurted.

Dad raised an eyebrow. "What does that mean?"

"I just . . . don't need a sleeping bag."

"Oh no, sweetheart, you absolutely do," Mom said. "Do you have one at home?"

"I don't know. Maybe."

I couldn't tell if my parents realized who Kenji was—the son of Dad's boss. If they knew, they'd definitely want Mr. Stillman's permission. Although probably they'd rather leave out Mr. Stillman completely.

"Mom, we have an extra sleeping bag, don't we?" I asked. "In the garage with all the fishing stuff?"

"Yes, but I already promised it to Ashlyn." Mom looked at Kenji with sympathy, but her voice was firm. "Kenji, please call home and ask your parents. You need their okay, and also a sleeping bag, or I'm afraid you can't stay here overnight."

My parents stood there like they refused to budge until Kenji called home. And Kenji realized it too, I guess, because he took his phone out of his pocket, fumbled with it for a bit, and typed something slowly.

"Okay," he said after a minute. "I asked. They don't always answer right away, so." He shrugged.

Mom and Dad exchanged a look.

"Well, I hope they'll answer by the time we get back," Dad said. He didn't make it sound like a deadline exactly, but I could tell my parents weren't going to let Kenji off the hook.

And from the way Kenji's shoulders slumped, I could tell Kenji knew it too.

INTERVIEW

Not long after my parents returned with the tents and the sleeping bags, a black SUV drove up, and Kenji's dad got out. I could tell it was Kenji's dad because he had the same floppy dark hair and the same shoulders-first way of walking. But it seemed strange how he was wearing a white shirt with a button-down collar and ironed-looking khaki pants—dressed like it was a workday, even though it was the Sunday of a three-day weekend.

The first thing he did was go over to Dad, who didn't seem shocked to see him. So that answered my question: yep, Dad definitely knew whose kid Kenji was.

"Oh no, it's our pleasure," Dad was telling him, smiling. "Great to see they're all friends."

Mr. Stillman dropped his head slightly and smiled back. What was going on here? I thought Kenji's dad was supposed to be a tyrant, a mean boss. And of course a polluter. So why were he and Dad both smiling, acting like everything was totally normal?

"All right, Kenji, time to go," Mr. Stillman called out.

Kenji was sitting under a tree next to Archer, who looked up from his phone.

"Kenji," Mr. Stillman said calmly. "Did you hear what I just said?"

Kenji still didn't move. Or look at his dad, who wasn't smiling anymore.

"Kenji, you should go," Em said.

"All right, *fine*." Kenji got up, stomped over to the black SUV, and slammed the car door behind him.

No one spoke for a few awkward seconds.

"Your son's a great kid," Dad said at last.

"Thanks, we think so," Mr. Stillman replied. "Well, thanks for letting Kenji spend the day with you all. Have a good evening, folks." He gave a quick wave, got in the car, and drove off. *VROOM.*

"Poor Kenji," Riley said.

I thought so too; the whole thing felt uncomfortable in

a way I couldn't explain. I mean, I could definitely imagine Kenji's dad, with his white shirt and his ironed pants, telling Kenji that guitars were a waste of time. Also that dogs weren't allowed, and even that the planet was doing just fine. But somehow Mr. Stillman wasn't what I expected. I'd pictured him as a cartoon villain in a trench coat, pouring acid into the water when no one was looking. But could he actually be an okay person?

Although why else would Kenji have behaved like that just now—almost like a bratty little kid? And his dad *did* say nasty stuff about Mr. Hendricks and the River Project. And stress out Dad at work. And even that reporter Lauren Bicks had suggested Gemba was dumping chemicals—

Ugh, that interview. Mr. Stillman had to know about it by now. Maybe he blamed Dad for what I'd said. Even though I didn't actually *say* it.

But if he did blame me, why was he acting so smiley with Dad?

Again it felt like my brain was a bouncy castle, with too many thoughts crashing around, over and over.

An hour later Min was unloading three large wicker picnic baskets from her Prius, explaining everything she'd made for us—spring rolls, tofu dumplings, spicy sesame noodles, and veggie tacos, plus brownies for dessert.

"You're going to eat this with us, right?" I asked her, grinning.

"Of course!" Min laughed loudly. "You think I'd cook all day and not share the meal?"

So I guess we'll do the interview afterward, I thought. *Okay, cool.*

Mom spread a couple of old blankets on the ground and we sat down for supper. Min was the kind of cook who criticized everything she made—this dish was too spicy, this one could have used a little more garlic—but seriously, all her food was incredible.

Even so, I could barely eat. Despite all the rehearsing in my head, the thought of a second interview made my stomach hurt. What if I messed up again? Embarrassed myself? Embarrassed other people? Blamed Gemba by accident? It was great that I'd have a second chance to explain things, but could I do a better job this time? It felt like an oral extra-credit report after I'd already failed a big test.

The dinner went on and on, with the grown-ups talking politics and gossip. Around eight o'clock, Em's parents showed up to get her, waiting in their car while she said endless goodbyes to everyone.

"Text me if you witness anything," she said in my ear. "But I don't think you will."

"Yeah, maybe not," I admitted.

"But it's still good you're doing this."

"You think so?"

"Yes, Haven, I do. Whatever happens, even if nothing does."

This time she actually did give me a hug, and I let her.

Then I went over to Min, who was loading the leftovers into her trunk.

"Is this a good time to talk?" I asked.

"Oh, of course, honey," she said. "You know I always love chatting with you! Just first grab that casserole dish, okay? Make sure the lid's on tight; I don't want garlic sauce all over the back seat."

I snapped the lid on tight. "Thanks so much for cooking all this. Everything was delicious."

"My pleasure. I hate cooking for myself, and Archer doesn't care about food; he could live on Doritos." Min laughed. "So what's up?"

"Um. Well, I'm ready for the interview."

"Interview? About what?"

"You know. Today. This protest."

Min stared at me like I was speaking Martian.

My stomach fluttered. "Didn't Archer tell you? I thought he did."

"Well, he called while I was in the middle of cooking. Maybe I didn't hear it right. Why don't you tell me yourself?"

I swallowed. "I guess I'm asking for a sort of do-over. I didn't like how my interview came out yesterday, and I thought maybe you could write a different one. About what we're doing here today. So people would understand—"

"Whoa, hold on a minute, Haven. What would the story be?"

"The story? I don't know. How we camped out to witness any dumping?"

"Did you? Witness any dumping?"

"Well, no. Not yet."

Her forehead wrinkled. "So what would I write? That a small group of kids and a few parents went camping and ate a delicious meal on picnic blankets?"

I didn't answer.

Min took my hands in hers. "Haven, I'm not just Archer's mom; I'm a professional journalist. And if I come to my editor with this story, I know exactly what he's going to say: 'Why am I reading this? Why should anyone? What's the significance?'"

"But you covered the RiverFest, didn't you? And that was basically just a big party!"

"The RiverFest was a town event, with hundreds of people attending, and a nice photo op on a holiday weekend. This is—well, what is it exactly?" She waved her arm in the direction of the picnic blankets. "Look, Haven, I know

what's in your heart, and I totally support what you're trying to accomplish here. But this protest, or campout, or
whatever we call it, is not a story I can submit to my editor,
okay? I'm very sorry."

She gave me a big warm hug, said something to Archer
about bug spray, waved goodbye to the grown-ups, and
drove away with her leftovers.

BREATHE

By the time we were ready for bed, I just wanted the whole thing to be over. Seriously, if only my family had been at the river, I'd have begged my parents to take us home. There was no point pretending anything else: the protest had been a disaster, fizzling out to nothing. Hardly anyone was left—only Mom, Dad, and Carter, Riley and her mom, Archer, and Ashlyn. And me.

"All right," Mom said, slipping into Belmont Buddies mode. "This is how we'll do it, everyone. Archer and Carter in the green tent. Ashlyn, Riley, and Haven in the blue. Grown-ups in the tan."

I pulled Mom aside. "Mom, why can't Archer be in my tent with Riley? I don't even know Ashlyn!"

"Haven, we can't have Ashlyn sharing a tent with Carter."

"Why not?"

Mom lifted her chin in the direction of Carter and Ashlyn, whose green head was resting on my brother's shoulder as they watched a movie on her iPad.

"Because they're *in high school*," Mom said quietly, smiling a little. "Okay?"

I felt like a moron.

"Whatever," I answered as I turned away. It was so strange to see my brother liking a girl, and even stranger to see a girl liking him back.

Around ten thirty Riley, Ashlyn, and I settled into our sleeping bags in Riley's tent. Riley was obviously excited to hang out with a ninth grader, chatting and giggling with Ashlyn about which they hated worse—mosquito bites or wasp stings, homework or exams, raisins or broccoli, getting your period or having a cold. The conversation went on and on until finally Riley started snoring.

But I never fell asleep. I just lay as still as I could, listening to insects vibrating in the night air. How many of them were as endangered as the honeybees? I supposed I could look it up if I wanted to take out my phone, but what would be the point of knowing, I asked myself, if I was this hopeless as an environmental activist? Ms. Packer had told me to focus on small things—but what small thing had I actually accomplished? I couldn't even get Min to write a second article, or take a photo of our posters.

I was the opposite of Kirima Ansong. She was brave and bold, a true leader in the world. And I was just . . . this kid. A twelve-year-old in a sour-smelling sleeping bag.

After an hour of staring at the top of the tent, it felt like I was suffocating. Riley and Ashlyn were both snoring, and I didn't want to wake them, so as quietly as I could, I slipped out of the sleeping bag and went outside to breathe.

A few feet away there was Carter, sitting on a big rock, watching something on his phone.

"Hey," I said softly.

He startled. "Oh. Hi, Haven. Why aren't you asleep?"

"Eh, I never sleep anymore; it's boring. Why aren't you?"

"I don't know. Archer wouldn't shut up about bugs."

"Yeah, he has a thing about them. Bug-phobia." I sat next to my brother. The rock felt cold and sharp on my butt. "Carter? Can I ask you something?"

"No." He turned off his phone. "All right, yes."

"What did you think about Kenji's dad?"

"Kenji's dad?" My brother scratched his nose. "I dunno. He seemed okay. A little tense, maybe."

"Yeah. But not evil, right?"

"Well." Carter thought for a bit. "I mean, you can't judge someone based on five minutes. And he's a big international businessman, right? So I'm sure he's good at acting friendly in public."

"I guess."

"And even if he's a tough dad or a tough boss, it doesn't mean he's a polluter. Although if he's nice, it doesn't mean he isn't." Carter stretched his legs. "We don't know the truth—about Gemba or Kenji's dad, or any of it, really. Maybe we never will."

I sighed. It was hard to accept that my brother was right. But in my heart I knew he probably was.

For a minute or two, we sat quietly in the dark.

"Can I ask something else?" I said.

"Is this a choice?"

"No, it's not. When we're grown-ups, what do you think Belmont will be like?"

"What do you mean? Like, will there be a different pizza place? Or a movie theater?"

"No. I mean with climate stuff. Will the whole town be underwater? Or maybe a big hurricane will pull up all the trees, or blow off everybody's roofs? Or we'll have one of those polar vortex things and everything will be buried in ice? Or the ice will melt all of a sudden, like the Doomsday Glacier—"

"Whoa, stop. You're way too cheerful for me, Haven."

"Carter, don't tease, okay? I'm really serious about this. And scared that nothing we do makes any difference."

"Sorry. And yeah, I'm scared too." He stood. "But nobody knows what's going to happen. All I can tell you is that a lot of governments are starting to listen to climate scientists. And maybe people will listen too."

"Before it's too late, you mean."

"Right. Before it's too late." He yawned loudly, the way you do only in front of family. "What time is it?"

"I dunno. I left my phone in the sleeping bag. Late."

Carter smooshed my hair. "But not *too* late," he said over his shoulder as he went into his tent.

For a while I sat by myself, listening to the crickets, counting the stars. Maybe there were constellations we didn't know about. Other worlds, other galaxies, too, where everything was safe and protected.

I never thought this way when I was in my bedroom, playing the alphabet game, staring at the ceiling when I couldn't sleep. But somehow, being outdoors at night, breathing the sweet, cool air, made me wonder. And for the first time in forever, I actually felt peaceful.

Finally I yawned too, and crawled back into our tent.

REPORT

How I Tried (and Failed)
to Save the Belmont River
by Haven Jacobs

Over the Memorial Day weekend I tried to organize a protest to save the Belmont River from toxic chemicals. The reason I wanted to do it was because of what my team observed in our River Project. I believe that toxic chemicals in the water may have caused the death of many pollution-sensitive macroinvertebrates, and possibly also

explain why there were no frogs. So I wanted to speak out against anyone who may be polluting our town's river.

In my opinion the protest failed in several ways:

—The first part of the protest was a "festival" held on Saturday that was supposed to focus the town on what's happening to the river. People cleaned up a bunch of litter that was in the water, but they barely paid any attention to the information table where we described our findings in the River Project. In addition, they made a lot more trash. Mostly this "festival" was a social thing that didn't actually communicate about chemicals in the water.

—Also on Saturday I gave a newspaper interview for the Belmont Bee that turned out very embarrassing. It should have been about the river, but it ended up being about my "eco-anxiety" with details that were EXTREMELY PERSONAL. It also referred to other kids in a way I didn't mean. The worst part is that it made it sound like I was accusing Gemba, which I did NOT do! Here is the link to the interview so you can see why I'm upset about it.

—I tried to get people to join me at the river on Sunday, but I guess I didn't think hard enough about what I was trying to achieve. It was kind of silly to *think we'd catch someone dumping chemicals in the river, especially on a holiday weekend! My brother Carter, who's in ninth grade, said we should have been demanding something specific, like a new law or a big investigation into who was polluting, and I think he was probably right.*

Also, I didn't plan a way to get our message out to the public, so even though we made signs (and had a chant), we didn't communicate anything to anybody else. I tried to get Min Zhang (Archer's mom) to write another article, but she said our Sunday protest wasn't really a story, because even though a lot of people showed up in the morning (thirty-seven!), the whole thing ended up being a sort of campout that most people skipped.

These are just some of the ways I believe I messed up as an environmental activist.

In this report I will describe a few of Kirima Ansong's protests and why they were much more successful than mine

"Haven?" Mom was standing in my bedroom door. "Supper's ready."

"I'm not hungry," I said.

"You're not? You feeling okay?" Immediately she was

touching my forehead with a cool hand. "Your skin feels a little warm, although I think it's just sunburn. What are you doing?"

"A report for Ms. Packer."

She frowned. "She assigned your class a report on a holiday weekend?"

"No, it's instead of all the homework I owe her. I promised I'd do it, and I don't want to mess up." *Mess up one more thing,* I thought.

Mom gave me a warm, soft hug. "Haven, honey, I know you're disappointed about this weekend. But you're in seventh grade; no one expects you to save the world. The best you can do is learn from this experience, and take that with you for next time."

"I guess," I said. "I mean, if there *is* a next time."

Mom kissed my hair. "Oh, there will be, sweet potato. I have no doubt about *that.*"

An hour later I emailed the report to Ms. Packer.

PRESENTATION

Ziggy *mrowed* in my face at five o'clock on Tuesday morning. This was good for two reasons. First, the fact that he woke me up meant that I'd actually been sleeping. And second, getting up so early meant I could make myself a bowl of Lucky Charms with orange juice without anyone awake to comment on it. I hardly ever got to have Lucky Charms for breakfast; when I did, I used OJ instead of chocolate milk, because it seemed more breakfasty.

I got to school about twenty minutes early, so I went to see Ms. Packer.

"I sent you my report last night," I said. "Seven and a half pages."

She smiled. "Yes, and I printed it so I could write comments. That was a lot of hard work, Haven."

"Yeah, it was." *Then please don't fail me,* I added in my head.

"Well, I thought it was excellent," she said.

"Really?"

"Yes, really." She handed it back to me, all stapled together. Right away, without even thinking, I flipped to the back page to see the grade. But there wasn't one. Just tons of comments in loopy purple ink.

Ms. Packer waited while I tried to read her handwriting. But my eyes wouldn't focus. Finally I just looked up.

She was watching me closely. "One thing I did want to mention—you spent a lot of time describing how you messed up. But you really didn't, you know, because you committed yourself to something you believe in strongly. And now you have experience to draw on in the future."

"That's kind of what my mom said," I admitted.

"Well, then we agree. The world needs kids like you, so don't give up, Haven." Ms. Packer pressed my shoulder. "Anyhow, I hope you got what you needed from this essay."

"Yeah, I guess I did, actually. Thanks for letting me do it."

"You let *yourself* do it." She smiled warmly. "Wanna hear another one of my favorite quotes? 'When the student is ready, the teacher appears. When the student is truly ready, the teacher disappears.'"

"Oh, but you didn't disappear," I said, smiling back. "I mean, I see you right there."

"I see you too, Haven Jacobs." She laughed. "By the way, I ran into Mr. Hendricks in the main office just now. He said he wants to talk to you as soon as possible."

"He *does*?"

Immediately my stomach knotted. Maybe I wasn't failing social studies anymore, but was I failing science now instead?

I went straight to his classroom. He was sitting at his laptop in the back of the room, drinking coffee out of a mug that said MOMENT OF SCIENCE. Today his tee said FLAT PLUTO SOCIETY. No end to Mr. Hendricks's collection of dad-joke science merch, it seemed.

"Um, excuse me," I said in the doorway.

He looked up. Right away his face brightened. "Haven," he said. "Just the person I was hoping to see."

Not what you'd say to someone failing your class, I couldn't help thinking.

"Come over here. I want to show you something," he said. He seemed excited, not just jumpy from caffeine.

I left my backpack on a chair and walked over.

Mr. Hendricks pointed to his monitor. All I saw were numbers. A string of decimals in long, skinny columns.

"I'm sorry, I don't know what this is," I said.

"It's a report from Dr. Lopez! Remember how she took samples from the river? Well, her lab at the college analyzed it, and they've identified trace amounts of hydrofluoric acid."

I shrugged. "Okay."

"Haven, it's the type of acid they use to make frosted glass."

"Wait, what?" Finally my brain had logged on. "You mean the type of acid they use at Gemba?"

"Possibly! We still don't have direct evidence implicating Gemba, and it's not the only chemical Dr. Lopez identified. But with this data here, I think we're good for our presentation."

Presentation? I just blinked.

"Sorry, Haven," Mr. Hendricks said. "I know I'm throwing a lot at you. But remember back at the beginning of the River Project, I told the class that every year we submit our results to the town board? Well, this year our results were so off that I decided it wasn't enough just to email them a report; I wanted to appear before the town board in person. And Dr. Lopez's data clearly shows that the Belmont River is polluted, whatever the source."

"Cool," I said because I didn't know what else to say.

"Haven, I'd really like you to be part of our presentation."

"Me? Oh no, I couldn't!"

"Why not?"

"I just." My brain was zinging like a housefly searching for an open window. "I mean, I'm not a scientist. I can't explain what Dr. Lopez did—"

"You don't have to. She'll be there herself."

"So then . . . why do you need *me*?"

"Because I think the town board should hear from a local kid. Especially one who feels these things strongly."

Feels?

Oh no. Here we go again. Haven's feelings.

I snapped my rubber band.

"Haven, I read that interview you did," Mr. Hendricks said gently. "In the *Belmont Bee*."

I swallowed. "And that's what you want me to talk about? My eco-anxiety?"

"I think the town board needs to hear the whole story, how climate stuff affects all of us in different ways. Dr. Lopez will describe the data, and I'll help, but it's important to speak to them in human terms. Especially about the emotional impact on kids."

Cold drops of sweat were leaking from my armpits, so

I pressed my arms against my sides. An oral report about my nails and my stomach. How much more humiliation could I take?

Mr. Hendricks waited a long minute. When I still didn't answer, he spoke quietly. "No pressure, okay? If you're not up for this, I completely understand. Public speaking is not in everyone's comfort zone."

"It's not *just* the public speaking. It's talking about personal things—" My voice broke; I couldn't continue.

"No, I get it, Haven. It's a lot to ask. Please forgive me."

The strange thing was that I didn't turn and run out the door.

I mean, I could have. Maybe should have.

But for some reason my legs wouldn't move. It was like my brain was yelling at me to escape, but my body had a different opinion.

What would Kirima Ansong do?

As soon as I asked this question, I knew the answer. After spending all of yesterday afternoon and evening researching Kirima's protests, I couldn't pretend not to know the answer. Just a year ago, Kirima gave a twenty-minute speech at the United Nations, begging all the leaders of the world to focus on climate change. If Kirima could go up to the mic with cameras going and flashbulbs popping, a zillion people all over the world listening to every word she said, how could I be too scared to talk to six grown-ups from my tiny town? Especially when the issue was this important.

Maybe I'd messed up the protest and the festival, and the interview, too. But this was a way to make everything come out okay. A way to make the grown-ups listen. *The world needs kids like you, so don't give up, Haven.*

I took a breath.

"Okay, I'll do it," I said.

CHANGE

Kenji showed up in homeroom as if nothing had happened over the weekend. He chatted with Riley and laughed with Archer about something on his phone. I had the strong sense that he didn't want to discuss his dad, or if they'd fought after they got home.

But right before lunch I asked him if we could talk in private for a second.

"What about?" he asked. His eyes looked nervous, like he thought I'd ask about a fight with his dad.

"Don't worry," I said. "It's just about me."

He followed me over to the lockers without talking.

As we faced each other, a strange thought slipped into my head: *Good thing no more zit constellation!* I mean, the condition of my forehead was totally irrelevant, obviously. Still, it was a relief not to feel gross at that exact moment.

"So what's up?" Kenji asked.

I blurted out what Mr. Hendricks had told me: how he wanted me to do the presentation. And how even though I'd be talking about personal things, embarrassing things, I thought I should force myself to do it, and maybe he could be there too? Because Kenji cared about the river—about the planet in general—more than anyone else I knew. I didn't want him to get in trouble with his parents, but—

"Sure," Kenji interrupted. "When is this thing?"

I told him I didn't know yet.

"Whenever it is, I'll go with you," he said.

For the rest of that day, I couldn't stop thinking about those three last words: *go with you.*

"Haven, you'll need something to wear," Mom said when I told my family at dinner.

I groaned. "I have plenty to wear."

"I mean decent clothes. Not jeans or leggings. And definitely not shorts!"

"Mom, the town board won't be looking at my knees!"

"Not the point," Dad said as he speared some broccoli with his fork. "It's always important to look the part. First rule of grown-up-hood."

"But I'm not going as a grown-up! That's the whole point: to tell them how *kids* feel about the river. And about what's happening to the planet!"

"Even so." Dad put down his fork. "You want them to take you seriously, don't you? And also they should feel respected."

"Dad, Haven is talking to them so that *she* feels respected," Carter argued. My brother's eyes met mine. It was strange to think that just a few weeks ago we were . . . well, not enemies, exactly, but definitely not allies.

And I thought: So much had changed lately, and not just with Carter. With my friends. With Em. With Kenji, too. Even with my teachers.

And then I thought this: Sometimes change was scary, like what was happening to the planet. But when it came to people—including older brothers—sometimes change could be kind of amazing.

BRACELET

The presentation was scheduled for Friday at four o'clock.

The afternoon before, I had a session with my therapist, April. I told her how nervous I was about speaking to the town board, how I was sure my mind would completely blank, the way it usually did for oral reports.

"Hmm," April said, nodding. "Why do you think public speaking makes you nervous?"

I shrugged. "I don't know. It just does."

"Have you tried that old trick—imagining the folks you're talking to are in their underwear?"

"Not really. And that's sort of gross, anyway."

She smiled. "Well, would you consider writing down what you want to say? That way if you do blank, you can just read from your notes."

I decided to try it. Even so, all Friday I was sick with nerves. Finally at lunch I went to the school library to practice the words I'd written on a sheet of loose-leaf paper: *Good afternoon, Mayor Castillo and the Belmont Town Board, and thank you for letting me speak here today. My name is Haven Jacobs, and I'm a seventh grader at Belmont Middle School....*

Mom came home early from work. I think she wanted to be sure I wore a skirt—like when it came to saving the planet, skirt-wearing even mattered.

She also offered to drive me over to the town hall, but I told her that with everything I was about to say about protecting the environment, it seemed wrong not to just walk.

"Good point." She smiled. "I'll walk with you, then."

"You don't have to," I said.

"I know, but I want to. Is that okay?"

I was so nervous about my speech that I agreed. And just before we left, she handed me a little box.

"What is this?" I asked.

"Well, usually people *open* boxes to find out," she said, smiling.

I took off the top. Inside was a thin silver bracelet with a tiny charm—a frog.

I looked up at Mom.

"I just thought that since your nails are healing, you might enjoy wearing something on your wrist besides rubber bands," she said. "Also, Dad and I wanted to give you a little present to remember this special day. Because we're so proud of you. You know that, right?"

I threw my arms around her. Yes, I knew that.

"Oh, and I promise it doesn't vibrate," she said, laughing.

At 3:55, we arrived at town hall. Mom asked if I wanted her to come in.

"Maybe it would be better if you didn't," I said. I couldn't explain why, but saying all that eco-anxiety stuff in front of her . . . somehow it just seemed like it would be harder.

If Mom's feelings were hurt, she didn't show it. "Call me when you're done, okay?" she said. "Go get 'em, sweet potato!"

Right away I spotted Kenji sitting cross-legged under a tree, reading a book. He didn't react to the "sweet potato" stuff, but obviously he'd heard it.

Ugh.

Already the loose-leaf paper with my speech was damp from my clammy hands.

"Mr. Hendricks is inside," Kenji said as he stuffed the book into his backpack. "You look nice, Haven."

"Uh, thanks." *No zit constellations, woo-hoo!*

The two of us walked inside without talking. A woman with glasses on the top of her head showed us into Conference Room 2A, a big beige-walled room with a long table in the front for the mayor and the board members. The rest of the room was nothing but metal folding chairs—all empty except for Mr. Hendricks and Dr. Lopez in the first row, and Ms. Packer in the back.

I hadn't known Ms. Packer would be here. Seeing her helped me breathe a little—but it also meant more people in the audience.

Mr. Hendricks turned and waved as we took seats behind him. He was wearing a blue button-down shirt and a jacket, not one of his regular Mr. Science tees. Dr. Lopez was dressed in a black pantsuit, but her hair was still pink. I couldn't help thinking it was a sort of dare: *You assume I'm not a serious scientist? Well, just wait.*

She nodded at me and went back to reading her notes.

That was when I noticed Min across the room, hunched over her laptop. I hadn't expected to see her, either, but of course it made sense she'd be here. After all, a presentation to the town board was a "story," even if our campout/protest wasn't.

By now my heart was pounding and my hands were so sweaty I had to wipe them on my skirt. At least I'd listened to April and written out my speech word for word. So even though this was technically an oral report, I wouldn't need to worry about blanking—unless they asked questions after I finished reading. Did Mr. Hendricks say they'd be asking questions? How was it possible I couldn't remember?

I reached for the rubber band, and my fingers found the frog charm instead.

"The meeting of the Belmont Town Board is called to order," announced one of the men behind the long table. He was wearing a black jacket, a white shirt, and a dark bow tie, and before I could control myself, this thought popped into my head: *He looks like a penguin.*

I cough-laughed into my hand.

"You okay?" Kenji asked quietly.

"Just nervous," I muttered. "I hate oral reports. Why is there a mic?"

"Maybe they show this on local TV?"

Sure enough, a guy was setting up a TV camera in the back of the room. *Oh, great,* I thought. Who knew how many people would watch this? Watch *me.*

Mr. Hendricks stood and walked over to the microphone. In a calm-sounding voice, he explained the River Project and how our results compared to the last three years. Then Dr. Lopez went. To be honest, I didn't under-stand most of her report, which was basically just num-bers, but I could see the town-board people—three men and three women, plus the mayor—taking notes as she spoke. One of the women, who wore a complicated scarf around her neck, even asked a few questions.

Then it was my turn.

I stood. *Run,* my brain flashed. *Now.*

Kenji poked my arm. "Go get 'em, sweet potato," he murmured.

What?

I burst out laughing. I couldn't help it; the combination of nerves and surprise was too much.

Mr. Hendricks turned to pop his eyes at me.

Don't blow this! I yelled at myself.

I closed my eyes, took a deep breath, and made my way to the front of the room.

THE ON SWITCH

he first thing I did was apologize for laughing.

"Sorry, I'm just nervous," I told Mayor Castillo. I'd seen him in photos, and in a few parades, but never this close-up. He had a little puff of hair on top, like he was walking under a tree one day and a tiny bird's nest fell on his head. Was it a toupee? Maybe he just had puffy hair. Whatever it was, I needed to stop staring at it.

"No need to be nervous," he was saying. "We're eager to hear from you today, Haven."

"Um, thank you." I held the loose-leaf paper with trembling fingers. But maybe because my hands were so sweaty, it was like the ink had turned into water, a giant gush of words that all ran together: *riverprojectenvironmentclimate-chemicalsanxiety* . . .

My eyes couldn't—wouldn't—focus. It wasn't possible for me to read this speech, even if it hadn't smeared.

Okay, now what?

My brain was empty. Like a vacuum cleaner had sucked up all my words.

Should I try to imagine them all in their underwear? Bleh, no.

Penguin Guy cleared his throat.

Mayor Castillo smiled kindly. "Haven, can you tell us about your interest in the river?"

I breathed—too loudly—into the mic. "My interest?"

"Yes. We understand you're one of Mr. Hendricks's students? And you're interested in the environment?"

"Well, I wouldn't use the word 'interested.'"

The mayor raised his eyebrows. "No?"

"Yeah, it's more like obsessed. Terrified."

Penguin Guy coughed into his mic. He traded a look with Scarf Lady. A look that said, *Uh-oh, here we go.*

Something about that look—not an eye roll exactly, but one of those private wordless conversations between grown-ups—flipped the On switch for me.

They don't want to hear from a kid?

Well, too bad. Because I have stuff to say!

So I started talking: about the video Mr. Hendricks had shown us—the melting glaciers, the penguins—then about the doomscrolling, the nail-and-stomach stuff, the problems with social studies. How I couldn't stop thinking about the missing frogs. How it felt like the world was ending, and people in charge weren't doing anything to save it.

"Someone told me this is called eco-anxiety," I said. "Which I guess means anxiety about environmental things? All I know is that I'm angry and scared about the planet, and the way it's getting destroyed. The way grown-ups are *letting* it get destroyed. A lot of kids feel this way, actually."

"Yes, I'm sure that's true." Scarf Lady rested her chin on her folded hands. "My son is in fourth grade, and he talks about the climate crisis constantly. He even has nightmares about it."

"So do I, although some nights I'm too worried to even sleep! All my friends are worried also. We're trying to deal with it as much as we can, but what we're really hoping is that you'll listen. And not just listen—*do* something. Because if we told you we were depressed, you'd try to solve it for us, right? You'd take care of us; you'd bring us to a doctor. So why won't you try to solve this, too?"

For a few seconds no one answered.

Finally the mayor did. "Yes, we hear you, Haven," he

said, nodding. "We know many kids are concerned about the environment, and not only here in Belmont. But of course, we grown-ups can't simply snap our fingers. Climate issues are huge and complex."

"But you have the power to do *something*, right? Like investigating, so we know who's polluting the river. Or maybe making new laws, so it doesn't happen again. That's why you're at that table! And why our parents voted for you." I pointed to the back of the room. "Ms. Packer's over there; she and Mr. Hendricks are my two favorite teachers. And one of the things she taught me this year is that if you can't do great things, you should do small things greatly."

Ms. Packer's eyes met mine. She was beaming.

And I kept going. "So I think if we could save our river, it would be kind of a small thing, right? I mean, it wouldn't save the planet, and it wouldn't solve the climate crisis. But it *would* make a big difference to our town." I fingered the bracelet. "Also, it would show kids that grown-ups care about us. That you're listening to us. And that you don't want to hand us a planet with zero frogs."

I talked for a few more minutes about the festival and the protest, and then the mayor said thank you, and it was over.

"Nice work," Mr. Hendricks said, beaming. Ms. Packer

fist-bumped me, and Dr. Lopez did a thumbs-up as she walked over to chat with the penguin-looking board member.

"Haven, that was awesome," Kenji said as the two of us left town hall. "You sounded amazing."

"I did?"

"Yeah, you didn't even seem nervous. It wasn't like an oral report at all."

"Thanks. I guess I was too mad to be nervous. And once I started talking, I couldn't stop." I peeked at him. "I'm really glad you came here with me, Kenji."

Kenji blushed. "So am I."

"But you better not call me sweet potato again," I added, grinning.

CELEBRATION

Afterward I felt zapped by lightning. I needed to move—not just stand in front of town hall like a baby, waiting for Mom to pick me up— so I walked home. Well, half walked, half ran.

As soon as I stepped into the kitchen, Mom and Dad gave me a big squeezy hug and announced that we needed to celebrate.

"Celebrate what?" I asked.

"Are you serious?" Now Carter was in the kitchen too. "Haven, you *brought it* to the town board!"

"How do you know?"

"Ms. Packer emailed us," Dad said. "She said the mayor was very impressed."

"Well, of course he was, because Haven is very impressive!" Mom smooched my cheek. "And I vote we go out to dinner!"

"Because you don't want to cook?" I teased her, laughing.

Mom laughed too. "True. But also because I think you deserve a party."

"We can go back to Mumbai Gardens if you like," Dad told me. "Go ahead, invite your friends."

"Can I invite Ashlyn?" Carter asked me.

"Sure, why not," I said as I texted Riley and Archer.

Then I thought of something.

I asked Riley: Hey, can I have Em's phone number? I want to invite her.

Riley texted me the number followed by 😊😊😊.

OMG YES, Em texted back.

Then I did a really brave thing. I asked Archer for Kenji's number, and I texted him, too.

A minute later Kenji texted back: Thanks for inviting me, Haven, but my parents want me to stay here for dinner and I don't want another fight 😔 I hope you have a good meal, and I hope we can do something else soon. Maybe I could play something for you on my guitar? Altho I shd prob practice some more first.

P.S. The mayor called my dad after the meeting. I couldn't hear much, but it sounded like the mayor was talking A LOT and my dad wasn't happy.

It was a great meal—even though everyone kept making a fuss about my speech at town hall, as if I'd done a Kirima Ansong–level thing, which of course I hadn't.

"Haven, I can't *believe* you told off the mayor," Em said.

"I didn't," I said. "I just spoke and he listened. He was actually nice." I told them about Kenji's text, how he'd said the mayor had talked to Kenji's dad afterward. "But we don't know what that even means," I added.

Em pressed her lips. "You're always so pessimistic, Haven. Try to be positive for once."

Carter caught my eye and smiled.

Just as the waiters brought some gulab jamun for dessert, Archer got a text from Min.

He poked me. "Mom wrote her article about the town-board meeting. You wanna see it?"

Did I? Suddenly I couldn't eat the sweet fried dumplings in front of me.

"Sure," I said.

Archer texted me the link. Min's article was long; I had to skim eight paragraphs to find my name at the end:

After presentations by Belmont Middle School science teacher Adam Hendricks and Parnassus County Community College Assistant Professor Dr. Ada Lopez, seventh-grade environmental activist Haven Jacobs addressed the board.

"I'm angry and scared about the planet, and the way we're letting it be destroyed," she said. "The way grown-ups are letting it happen. A lot of kids feel this way, actually."

Saving the Belmont River, she continued, "wouldn't save the planet, and it wouldn't solve the climate crisis, but it would make a big difference to our town. Also, it would show kids that grown-ups care about us."

Ms. Jacobs explained how she organized protests this past weekend to spread awareness about chemicals in the Belmont River.

After the meeting adjourned, Mayor Ernesto Castillo commented: "I take this personally. The river is an important part of our town's identity. Our town government is fully committed to restoring the Belmont River to health, and we will take all measures necessary."

He added that he was moved by Ms. Jacobs's presentation. "We all need to listen better to our kids. They're hurting, because the planet is hurting. After all, it's their planet; we're just minding it for a little while."

Mayor Castillo would not specify which measures the town would take to address concerns about the river. However, two hours after the town board's meeting, local business Gemba Industries issued this statement: "As citizens of this town and stewards of this planet, we are committed to working with Belmont's town board to address the health of our environment. We condemn all illegal dumping of substances in the Belmont River and will vigorously assist any investigation."

Investigation? When I got to that word, my brain exploded.

All the mayor had said was that he would "take all measures necessary." Did that mean there'd be an investigation into Gemba? Maybe it did!

Anyway, it had to mean *something* that Gemba had made a statement like this—not admitting they were guilty, but also not saying they weren't! And obviously they knew that the mayor was watching them now. That the whole town was!

I was so happy, I took an extra dumpling.

BIG NEWS

The last week of school was a bunch of exams and projects you don't want to hear about, I'm sure. The main thing was I filled in every answer on my social studies final, and ended up with a seventy-one. Which meant I passed—although by then I didn't actually think Ms. Packer would fail me.

A few days later school ended, and two big things happened.

The first was that Dad quit his job at Gemba. Not because he thought Gemba was guilty, he told Carter and me, but because he got a better offer from another factory ten miles away. Better hours, better salary, and the boss was really nice, he said. Switching to this new job made total sense, but I couldn't help wondering if there was some other reason he wasn't saying.

The second thing was that Archer and Min showed up at my house in the middle of the afternoon.

"Breaking news!" Min shouted as Mom and I led them into the kitchen.

"You want some iced tea?" Mom asked. "Or a Diet Coke?"

Min waved her hand like she was swatting a fly. "No thanks, Heather! We came over to tell Haven about my reporting. Before it's in the *Belmont Bee* tomorrow morning."

"Wait till you hear this, Haven," Archer said.

"Just tell me," I begged.

"Sooo," Min said, "two days ago I learned that Petersburgh Pharmaceuticals, about twenty-five miles from here, had a big chemical accident back in March. An antibiotic they use to treat ear infections—it's called acetic acid—accidentally spilled into the Petersburgh River! Which feeds into the Belmont River!"

"Wait, what?" I stared at Min, then at Archer, and then at Carter, who'd come into the kitchen. "You mean *that's* how the Belmont River got polluted? It wasn't because of Gemba?"

"Not what I said." Min's voice was sharp. "Haven, you need to listen more carefully!"

Archer shot me a look: *See what my mom is like?*

"I don't understand," I said weakly.

Min folded her arms across her chest. "No one's saying Gemba *doesn't* have a role here, okay? And the statement they made after the town-board meeting strongly suggests they *do* have some culpability. But apparently, they're not the *only* factor."

Archer was smiling at me now. "Mom thinks the accidental spill got discovered because of what *you* said at the town board."

"What *I* said?" It felt like my jaw was unhinged, and my mouth was just hanging open. "But I didn't—"

"Your presentation with Mr. Hendricks and Dr. Lopez definitely got the ball rolling," Min said. "Wheels are turning, Haven, big wheels! The mayor is all over this; that's probably why Gemba issued their statement. And now the investigation is spreading across the region, which is how the Petersburgh spill got reported. So who knows what else they'll find."

"Yeah, there could be other polluters too," Archer said. "Maybe a lot of them!"

"Possibly, but we don't *know* that," Min said, flashing her eyes at him.

"Whoa," Carter said. "You think if Gemba *was* dumping toxic chemicals, they made the Petersburgh spill even worse? Or maybe the other way around?"

"Not my department," Min said, flicking her hand again. "That's a question for the environmental experts doing the investigation, and possibly Dr. Lopez. But yes, I'm wondering about that too. Toxic chemicals mixing with other toxic chemicals—how could it *not* be dangerous?"

Nobody spoke. We all watched as Ziggy wandered into the kitchen and lapped up water from his bowl. Faucet water, clean and safe.

Suddenly Min turned to Mom. "Actually, you know what, Heather? Iced tea sounds perfect. As long as it's very sweet."

After Min's article appeared in the *Belmont Bee* the next morning, I guess I expected something dramatic—TV satellite trucks in front of town hall, cameras flashing, reporters demanding answers from Mr. Stillman.

But nothing like that ever happened. By the end of that week, Belmont emptied out for the summer, just like normal. Archer left to spend a few weeks with his dad, the way he did every June. Em's family took a vacation—kayaking somewhere, I think. And Kenji went to Japan with his parents. But he'd be back in the fall, he said.

"So you miss him?" Riley teased as we walked through town one afternoon.

I stuck out my tongue, blue from Italian ice.

"Come on, Haven, don't deny it," she said. "You obviously *like* him."

"Where'd you get that from?"

"Your face! You can never hide anything."

So finally I just admitted it to Riley. "But it's totally pointless anyway," I added, "because he's in Japan now, and I bet he's never coming back to Belmont."

Riley slapped my arm. "Em's right. You *are* pessimistic, Haven."

But I didn't *want* to be pessimistic. About Kenji. Or the river. Or the planet. Or anything else, really.

I reminded myself what Min had said: Balls were rolling, wheels were turning. Just because I couldn't see those balls and wheels didn't mean things weren't happening. Good things.

I licked my blue ice. "Well, Kenji does owe me a song on his guitar," I said, not even trying to hide my smile.

PICNIC

Way too soon, it was the end of August. I hadn't done much all summer, just some cat-sitting and plant-watering when neighbors went away for vacation. Now everyone was back in town, except for Kenji, who'd told Archer he'd be returning to Belmont sometime around Thanksgiving. School was just a day away, and we knew what that meant: in eighth grade the teachers piled on work "to prepare kids for high school," they said. So all of us were feeling pretty down.

"What we need is a picnic," Em announced. By this

time I had to admit that she was a friend, even though sometimes she could be annoying.

And I agreed: a picnic sounded excellent.

We met at the river. Em's parents ordered us pizza and soda. Min had adopted a rescue puppy over the summer to keep her company while Archer was at his dad's, so Archer brought him along—a floppy-eared mutt named Stanley. Em and Riley threw a tennis ball for Stanley to fetch. Half the time it landed in the water, and Stanley would go galumphing after it, shaking river water all over us every time he came out.

"Stanley is worse than Xavier," Riley said as she nibbled her pizza crust. "Remember how he kept splashing when we did the River Project?"

"Yeah, that was really bad," I said.

"But *you* were happy, because you teamed with Kenji, right?"

"Shut up, Riley," I said, hiding my smile from Archer.

The picnic was fun. Riley played songs on her iPad and danced with Em. I even let Em drag me over to dance with them a little. Then I sat in the shade with Archer, who rubbed Stanley's belly as he described a new dumb game he was playing.

Everything felt like it always had, like normal. Was normal good or bad? *Maybe both,* I told myself.

"You all right?" Em asked as she plopped down beside me.

"Yeah, just quiet," I answered.

She pressed her lips. "Come on, Haven, don't lie. I know that look."

"So do I," Riley said.

Archer smooshed Stanley's ears. "We *all* do."

"Okay, fine," I said. "I was thinking how you can stare at the water all day and not see what's really happening. I mean, without high-tech equipment. And doesn't it feel the same with this investigation? Like we worked so hard, and we still can't tell if we've made any difference."

Archer flashed his eyes just like Min. "How can you say that, Haven? You read my mom's article! That other chemical company's in trouble. And Gemba made a statement!"

"I mean, yes, all that's definitely good." I tugged on my bracelet. "And I'm happy about it, I really am. Although I hope it's not just words. I hope they'll actually *do* something."

"Oh, I bet they will," Riley said. "Because everyone's paying attention now. Finally!"

"Right, and not just kids." I threw a stone in the water. "But don't you wish we knew something for sure?"

"Like what?" Em demanded.

"I don't know," I said. "A sign we actually *accomplished* something. I don't mean solved climate change or anything, just made one specific difference. Especially to the river."

No one spoke. I threw another stone into the river and watched it disappear.

Finally Archer announced that he needed to take Stanley home for supper.

"No, don't leave," Em begged, maybe because that meant the day was ending. "Just feed him pizza!"

Archer stood. "Can't. Stanley needs special kibble. The vet says he has a sensitive stomach."

"Yeah, I should be heading back too," Riley said. Her shoulders drooped.

I tossed my pizza crust in the garbage can and took a last sip of Coke. So this was it, then: the last scrap of summer. Starting tomorrow, everything would be the eighth-grade version of Lewis and Clark, but with even more homework. And no Ms. Packer or Mr. Hendricks. Or Kenji, either, for the next few months.

We all hugged each other.

And then.

Just as the hugs were ending, I heard it, or thought I did. A sound so faint I wasn't sure if I'd imagined it.

But no, there it was again. A twangy sound, like the

lazy snap of a thick rubber band. Or maybe a guitar.

Archer heard it also—he was grinning now.

So were Riley and Em.

And me. I was grinning too.

"Ribbit," said the frog.

ACKNOWLEDGMENTS

Infinite thanks once again to my brilliant editor, Alyson Heller, and to the whole Aladdin family: Valerie Garfield, Kristin Gilson, Michelle Leo, Amy Beaudoin, Nicole Benevento, Nia Todd, Olivia Ritchie. Karen Sherman, thank you for another terrific job of copyediting. Heather Palisi, thank you for the beautiful design.

Erika Pajarillo, special thanks for another gorgeous cover illustration.

I'm so lucky to work with Jill Grinberg and her all-star literary agency—especially Denise Page, Sam Farkas, and Sophia Seidner. You're the best.

Grateful for the expertise and passion of Media Masters Publicity—Tracey Daniels, Karen Wadsworth, and Casey Blackwell.

Eliza Hawthorne, thanks for careful reading and researching.

Thanks to the educators who generously shared their knowledge about stream studies: Dr. Hope Braithwaite, Assistant Professor of Watershed Quality of Utah State University; Ms. Annie Madden and Mr. Patrick Liu of Robert E. Bell School, Chappaqua, NY; and Mr. Archer

Carlucci of Ossining High School, Ossining, NY. Of course, all errors are my own.

As always, endless love and gratitude to my family—Chris, Josh, Lizzy & Jamie, Alex & Dani. Bonus thanks to my in-house readers/editors, Chris and Lizzy. I couldn't do this without your expert eyes (and ears). Lizzy, any writer is lucky to have you as an editor.

Sometimes kids ask me where I get my ideas. I tell them that my ideas usually come from my own life—not so much the specific details or events, but the emotions I felt growing up. This book is different, because when I was a kid, we didn't worry about the climate crisis, or wonder about the future of the planet. So my idea for this book came from listening to kids. We grown-ups have a lot to learn.

ABOUT THE AUTHOR

BARBARA DEE is the author of thirteen middle-grade novels published by Simon & Schuster, including *Violets Are Blue, My Life in the Fish Tank, Maybe He Just Likes You, Everything I Know About You, Halfway Normal,* and *Star-Crossed.* Her books have earned several starred reviews and have been named to many best-of lists, including the Washington Post Best Children's Books, the ALA Notable Children's Books, the ALA Rise: A Feminist Book Project List, the NCSS-CBC Notable Social Studies Trade Books for Young People, and the ALA Rainbow Book List Top Ten. Barbara lives with her family, including a naughty cat named Luna and a sweet rescue hound dog named Ripley, in Westchester County, New York.